BIG RED

BIG RED

By JIM KJELGAARD

Illustrations by Bob Kuhn

GROSSET & DUNLAP · NEW YORK

CONTENTS

BIG RED

IRISH SETTER

THE BULL DANNY WAS TRAILING HAD TRAVELLED SLOWLY for the last mile. Danny mounted a little knob, where the bull had apparently stopped, and looked ahead. The next tracks were eight feet beyond. From that point the bull had run. Danny raised the thirty-thirty carbine to his shoulder, and slipped the safety off. When he went forward again he walked slowly and quietly. For he knew that here the bull had scented Old Majesty, and started to run for his life.

Forty feet farther on, the tracks of a monster bear emerged from the beeches and joined those of the bull. Danny knelt, and laid his spread hand in the bear's paw mark. The imprinted track was longer and wider than his hand. Old Majesty! Danny rose and skulked on, careful to break no twig, rustle no leaf, and make no other noise that might reveal his coming. A hundred times he had stalked this great bear whose name had become a legend. But this time he might get the shot that he had so long awaited. Then, a hundred feet ahead, Danny saw what he was looking for.

The bull lay on its back in a little forest glade. Its head was twisted grotesquely under its body, and one lifeless foreleg thrust crookedly upward. Danny stood still, peering through the trees for some sign of the monster bear that had won another victory against the human beings with whom it was eternally at war. But all he saw was the wind-rustled trees and the dead bull. The bear, with his customary cunning, had put a safe distance between himself and the dangerous rifle in Danny's hands.

Danny went forward, and looked down at the fine young Holstein. The bull's neck had been broken by a single blow from a sledge-hammer paw, and there was a hole in its belly where Old Majesty had started to eat.

"Wonder how Mr. Haggin'll like this," Danny murmured to himself. "Another bull gone."

He looked again at the bull, dead scarcely ten minutes and fifteen hundred pounds of good beef. But it was Mr. Haggin's, not his. Still, it would be a neighborly act to see that it didn't spoil. Danny bled the bull, and ripped its belly open with a knife so it wouldn't bloat. Keeping the rifle ready, for he was afraid of the bear, he backed away from the bull's carcass and started off through the beeches.

With the shuffling, loose-kneed gait of the born woodsman he walked mile after mile, through the beeches, past the clearing where, by the grace of Mr. Haggin, he and his father were allowed to live, over the bridge at Smokey Creek, and on to the edge of Mr. Haggin's Wintapi estate. Danny stopped there. He had seen it before. But the sight of such luxury never failed to impress him and was always worth another look.

Mr. Haggin's carefully nurtured acres stretched as far as the eye could see. Thoroughbred cattle grazed in the elaborately fenced pastures, and blooded horses snorted in the paddocks. Mr. Haggin's gray barns, big as all the other barns in the Wintapi put together, rose in the center of the estate and beside them were the six miniature mansions Mr. Haggin had built for the families of the six men who worked his farms. Mr. Haggin's house, a huge, white-gabled one protectively surrounded by imported blue spruces, was some distance from all the rest. Danny eyed it, then forgot everything but the red dog that was coming toward him.

A shining, silky red from nose to tail, the dog was trotting up the path Danny was walking down. His eyes were fixed on Danny, and his tail wagged gently a couple of times. Ten feet away he stood still, his finely chiselled head erect and his body rigid. Spellbound, Danny returned the dog's gaze. He knew dogs, having owned and hunted with hounds since he was old enough to do anything. The red dog was not a hound—Danny knew vaguely that it was called an Irish setter—but never before had he seen any dog that revealed at first glance all the qualities a dog should have. Danny walked forward, and knelt to ruffle the red dog's ears.

"Hi boy," he said. "How are you, Red?"

The red dog quivered, and raised a slender muzzle to sniff Danny's arm. For a moment Danny petted him, then straightened up. When callers came visiting him, he didn't like his hounds played and tampered with. It spoiled them, made them harder to handle. And certainly Mr. Haggin wouldn't want this red dog played with either. When Danny walked on the red dog kept pace, walking beside and looking up at him. Danny pretended not to notice, and went straight to the horse barn where Robert Fraley, Mr. Haggin's overseer, was directing two grooms who were saddling two restive horses. Robert Fraley hailed him.

"What do you want?"

Danny stiffened. Sometimes he just didn't like the way that Fraley acted, as though he owned the place and Danny was just dirt under his feet. And his business was with Mr. Haggin.

"I want to see Mr. Haggin," he said.

"He'll be down in a few minutes. Here, Boy."

Robert Fraley snapped his fingers, and the red dog crouched closer to Danny's knees. Danny watched understandingly. The dog wasn't afraid. But he wanted to stay near Danny, and there was a regal something in his manner that told Robert Fraley he was going to stay there. Danny folded his arms and stared stonily out across Mr. Haggin's meadows. He saw Mr. Haggin and another man leave the house, but turned his head in affected surprise when they had come near. Mr. Haggin, a crisp, clipped man in his early fifties, said,

"Hello, Danny."

"Howdy, Mr. Haggin. I found your bull."

"Where?"

"Dead, up on Stoney Lonesome. That big bear got him."

Mr. Haggin looked angry. The big red dog rose, and walked courteously over to greet his master. He returned to Danny.

"Put him back in his kennel, will you, Bob?" Mr. Haggin said.

Robert Fraley grasped a short whip and came over to seize the dog's collar. The red dog strained backwards, and fire leaped in Danny's eyes. He had seen what Mr. Haggin had not. Robert Fraley had twisted the red dog's collar, and hurt him. But the dog would not cry out.

"Can't something be done about that bear?" Mr. Haggin was asking irritably. "He's killed five cattle and nineteen sheep for me so far, and every one a thoroughbred."

"Pappy's been gunnin' for him ten years," Danny said simply. "I been after him myself for five, sinst I turned twelve years old. He's too smart to be still-hunted, and hounds are afraid of him."

"Oh, all right. Here's your two dollars. I'll call on you the next time anything goes astray, Danny."

Danny pocketed the two one-dollar bills. "The beef lies on Stoney Lonesome," he volunteered.

"I'll see that it's brought in." Mr. Haggin and the other man walked toward the horses, but Mr. Haggin turned around. "Was there something else, Danny?"

"Yes," Danny said recklessly. "What's that red dog of yours good for, Mr. Haggin?"

"Boy? Champion Sylvester's Boy? He's a show dog."

"What's a show dog?"

"It's—it's sort of like a rifle match, Danny. If you have the best dog in the show you get a blue ribbon."

"Do you waste a dog like that just gettin' blue ribbons?" Danny blurted.

Mr. Haggin's eyes were suddenly gentle. "Do you like that dog, Danny?"

"I sort of took a fancy to him."

"Forget him. He'd be lost in your woods, and wouldn't be worth a whoop for any use you might have for a dog."

"Oh sure, sure. By the way, Mr. Haggin, what's the money cost of a dog like that?"

Mr. Haggin mounted his horse. "I paid seven thousand dollars," he said, and galloped away.

Danny stood still, watching the horsemen. A lump

rose in his throat, and a deadening heaviness enfolded him. Throughout his life he had accepted without even thinking about them the hardships and trials of the life that he lived. It was his, he was the man who could cope with it, he could imagine nothing else. But since he had started playing with his father's hound puppies a great dream had grown within him. Some day he would find a dog to shame all others, a fine dog that he could treasure, and cherish, and breed from so that all who loved fine dogs would come to see and buy his. That would be all he wanted or needed of Heaven.

Throughout the years he had created an exact mental image of that dog. Its breed made little difference so long as it met all the other requirements, and now he knew that at last his dream dog had come to life in Champion Sylvester's Boy. But seven thousand dollars was more than he and his father together had earned in their entire lives.

Danny looked once at the kennel where Robert Fraley had imprisoned the red dog, and resolutely looked away. But he had seen the splash of red there, an eager, sensitive dog crowding close to the pickets that confined him. If only Red was his . . . But he wasn't and there was no way of getting him.

With his right hand curled around the two crisp, new bills in his pocket, Danny walked slowly across Mr. Haggin's estate to the edge of the beech woods. He stopped and looked back. Mr. Haggin's place stretched like a mirage before him, something to be seen but never touched. Anything on it was unattainable as the moon to one who lived in a shanty in the beech woods, and made his living by hunting, trapping, and taking such odd jobs as he could get. And seven thousand dollars was an unheard-of sum to one who knew triumph when he captured a seventy-five-cent skunk or weasel pelt.

Danny walked on up the shaded trail that led to his father's clearing. It wasn't rightly his father's; he owned it by squatter's rights only, and Mr. Haggin had bought up all the beech woods clear back to Two Stone Gap. But Mr. Haggin had said that they might live there as long as they chose provided that they were careful not to start any fires or cut any wood other than what they needed for fire wood, and Danny reckoned that that was right nice of Mr. Haggin.

The log bridge over Smokey Creek was suddenly before him. Danny walked to the center, and stood leaning on the rail and staring into the purling creek. He seemed to see the red dog's reflection in the water, looking up at him with happily lolling tongue, waiting Danny's word to do whatever needed doing. And he could do anything because a dog with his brains could be taught anything. He . . . he was almost human.

The image faded. Danny walked on up the trail to where his father's unpainted frame house huddled in the center of a stump-riddled clearing. Asa, the brindle mule, grazed in the split-rail pasture and the Pickett's black and white cow followed Asa about. Four bluetick hounds ran to the ends of their chains and rose to paw the air while they welcomed Danny with vociferous bellows. Danny looked at them, four of the best varmint hounds in the Wintapi except that they were afraid of Old Majesty. But they were just ordinary varmint hounds. Danny went up and sat down on the porch, leaning against one of the adze-hewn posts with his eyes closed and his long black hair falling back on his head. Three lean pigs grunted about his feet. The hounds ceased baying.

Just before sunset his father came out of the woods. A wooden yoke crossed his shoulders, and a galvanized pail swung from either end of the yoke. He wiped the sweat from his head and eased the pails down on the porch.

"Forty pounds of wild honey," he said with satisfaction. "It'll bring eight cents a pound down to Centerville."

Danny sat up and peered into the sticky mess that the pails contained.

"Shouldn't you ought to of waited until fall?" he asked. "There would of been more in the tree."

"Sure now," Ross Pickett scoffed, "any time your pappy can't find a honey tree you'll see white crows a-flyin' in flocks. They'll be more, come fall."

"I reckon that's right," Danny admitted. "You hungry?"

"I could eat."

Danny entered the house and stuffed kindling into the stove. He poured a few drops of coal oil on it, and threw a match in. When the fire was hot he cooked side pork, and set it on the table along with fresh bread, wild honey, milk, and butter. Ross Pickett ate silently, with the ravenous attention that a hungry man gives to his food. When they had finished both sat back in their chairs, and after a suitable interval Danny asked,

"What's a show dog?"

"I don't rightly know," Ross Pickett said deliberately. "Near's I can come to it, it's a dog that's got more for shape than anything else. They got to be the right distance between their hocks and ankles, their tail's got to droop just right, and every hair on 'em's got to be in the right place."

"What they good for?"

Ross shrugged. "Rich people keeps 'em. What you drivin' at, Danny?"

"A dog," Danny breathed. "Such a dog as you never saw before. He looks at you like he was lookin' right through you. The color and line that dog's got, and the brains . . . ! It would be worth workin' a hundred years to own a dog like that. Mr. Haggin owns him, and he cost seven thousand dollars."

Ross Pickett's eyes lit up. Then his face sobered and he shook his head.

"Forget it," he admonished. "Mr. Haggin's been mighty good to us. We don't want him mad at us, and he would be if ever we brought trouble to one of his dogs. Besides, he wouldn't be no good if he's a show dog."

"I saw him," Danny insisted. "I should know what he's good for."

"Forget him," Ross Pickett ordered.

Night fell, and Danny went to his cot. For a long while he listened to the shrieking whip-poor-wills outside.

Finally he fell into a light sleep that was broken by dreams of a great red dog that came up to smell his arm and retreated tantalizingly out of reach. The dog came again, but always ran just as Danny was about to seize it. Finally it climbed a tree, and Danny had climbed halfway after it when a great wind began to shake the tree. Danny rolled sleepily over, and awoke to find Ross shaking his shoulder. His father was excited, breathless, afraid.

"Danny!" he panted. "Wake up! That dog of Mr. Haggin's, the one you talked about! Danny, it followed you home and it's a-layin' outside on the porch now! Get up and take it back! Quick, before Mr. Haggin misses it! We'll have every police in the county after us!"

Danny pulled on his trousers, draped a shirt over his shoulders, and went to the door. Morning mists hovered over the clearing. The black and white cow heaved herself humpily from her couch by the haystack and Asa drooped his head in the lee of the barn. Lying on the porch's edge was the red dog. He rose and wagged his tail. There was dignity in his greeting, and uncertainty, as though, after having spent most of his life as a scientific plaything, the dog did not know exactly how he would be received by this new person to whom he had come for the companionship that he craved. Danny knelt, and snapped his fingers.

"You come a-visitin', Red?" he crooned. "Come here, Red."

The dog walked over and laid his head on Danny's shoulder. Danny rubbed the silky coat, and squeezed the dog ecstatically. Red whimpered, and licked his face.

"Danny!" Ross Pickett said frantically, "take that dog back to Mr. Haggin! I'm goin' in the woods so nobody won't think I tempted it up here!"

"All right," Danny said meekly.

He watched his father, with the honey pails on the yoke and his bee-hunting box in his pocket, stride swiftly across the clearing and disappear into the forest. Danny looked down at the dog, and tried to brush from his mind a thought that persisted in staying there. He had always dreamed of having a dog like this as his constant companion. That, of course, was impossible. But Red could be his for the day. Mr. Haggin might put him in jail or something, but it would be worth it. No, he'd better not. He'd better take him right back.

But it seemed that, once started, his feet just naturally strayed away from the trail over the Smokey Creek bridge. That was bothersome at first, and Danny veered back toward the trail. Then after a while he no longer cared because he knew that this one day out of his life would be worth whatever the penalty for it might be. He was afield with a dog that lived up to his grandest dreams of what a dog should be. Besides, Danny felt resentment toward Mr. Haggin, the money-blinded man who would use a dog like this only for winning blue ribbons.

For Danny had been right and Mr. Haggin wrong. Red—that hifalutin' handle Mr. Haggin had used was no proper title for a dog—was a natural hunter. He swept

into a thicket, and came to a rigid point. Danny walked
forward, and two ruffed grouse thundered up. But the
dog held his point. Danny knelt, and patted his head.

"You've sure seen birds before this," he said.

But, even if Red had been the most blundering fool
in the woods, Danny knew that it still would have made
no difference. Good hunting dogs were plentiful enough
if you knew where to find them, or wanted to take
enough time to train them. But a dog with Red's heart
and brain—there just weren't any more. Danny looked
at the sun and regretted that two hours had already
passed. This day would be far too short. With nightfall
he simply must take Red back to Mr. Haggin.

They wandered happily on, and climbed the ridge up
which Danny had trailed the straying bull yesterday.
Red came in to walk beside him, and Danny turned his
steps toward the dead bull. If Mr. Haggin hadn't yet
sent someone to get it, it was a sure sign that he didn't
want it. Danny and Ross could feel perfectly free at
least to come take the bull's hide. Danny broke out to
the edge of the glade, and the red dog backed against
his knees with bristling hackles and snarling fangs.
Thirty steps away Old Majesty stood with both fore-
paws on his kill. Majesty the wise, the ruler of these
woods, too smart to be shot and smart enough to know
that Danny carried no gun. The outlaw bear rose on his
hind legs, swinging his massive forearms. Danny shrank
against a tree, awaiting the inevitable charge. Old
Majesty was about to settle once and for all their long-
standing feud.

The red dog barked once, and flung himself across the clearing straight at the bear. Danny wanted to shriek at him not to do it, to come back because the bear would certainly kill him. But his tongue was a dry, twisted thing that clung to the roof of his mouth, and he could utter no sound. For one tense moment the bear stood his ground. Then he dropped to all fours, and with Red close behind him, disappeared in the forest.

Danny probed the forest with his eyes, and strained his ears, but could neither see nor hear anything. He turned and ran, back down Stoney Lonesome and through the beech woods to his father's clearing. He flung himself inside the cabin, snatched up his gun and a handful of cartridges, and ran back. For five minutes he stood by the dead bull, watching and listening.

But the forest had swallowed both bear and dog.

Danny tried to stifle the panic that besieged him. It was no longer fear of Old Majesty, or of Mr. Haggin and anything he might do, but he was afraid for Red. When Old Majesty had drawn him far enough away he would certainly turn to kill him. Danny suppressed a sob and went forward to find their trail.

He found it, leading out of the glade straight toward the back reaches of the Wintapi. Running hard, the bear had bunched his four feet together and scuffed the leaves every place he struck. Danny ran, hating the sluggishness of his feet and the snail's pace at which they carried him. It was his best speed, but the dog and bear were travelling three times as fast. A mile from the glade he found where the bear had slowed to a trot, and a half mile beyond that where he had turned for the first time to face the pursuing dog.

A huge, knobby-limbed beech raised at the border of a bramble-thick patch of waste land, and the bear had whipped about with his back to the trunk. Danny's heart was leaden as he looked about for tell-tale mats of red hair or drops of blood. But all he saw was the plainly imprinted tale of how the red dog had come upon and charged the bear. Old Majesty had left his retreat by the beech tree, and with whipping front paws had tried to pin the red dog to the earth. Red had danced before him, keeping out of reach while he retreated. A hundred feet from the tree the bear, afraid to leave his rear exposed while a dog was upon him and a man might come, had gone back. Red had charged again, and once more had danced away from the bear's furious lunges. Then the bear had left the tree.

"He smelt me comin'," Danny whispered to himself. "Red, you're sure playin' your cards right. If only I can stay close enough to keep him runnin', to keep him from ketchin' you . . ."

But tracking over the boulders was painfully slow work. Sweat stood out on Danny's forehead while, by a broken bramble, a bit of loosened shale, or an occasional paw print between the boulders, he worked out the direction that Old Majesty had taken. The sun reached its peak, and began slowly to sink toward its bed in the west. Danny clenched his hands, and wanted to run. But he knew that by so doing he would lose the trail. And, if he did that, Red would be forever lost too.

The first shades of twilight were darkening the forest when Danny finally crossed the boulders and was again among trees. He found the bear's trail in the scuffed leaves there, and with his rifle clutched tightly to him ran as fast as he could along it. Old Majesty had climbed straight up the long, sloping nose of a hump-backed ridge and had run along its top. Then he had dipped suddenly down into a stand of giant pines. Black night overtook Danny there. He bent over, painfully picking out each track and following it. When he could no longer do that, he got down on his hands and knees and tried to follow the trail by feeling out each track. But that was impossible.

"Keep your head, Danny," he counselled himself. "You can't do nothin' in the night."

He sat down with his back against a huge pine, straining his ears into the darkness for some bark or snarl, something that might tell him where the bear had gone. But there was only silence. A dozen times he started up to peer hopefully about for dawn. But the night was a thousand hours long. Not able to sleep, he sat against the tree looking into the night-shrouded maze of lost valleys and nameless canyons into which the bear had gone. Then, after an eternity, a gray shaft of light dropped through one of the pines to the needle-littered earth. Danny leaped to his feet. By bending very close to the earth he could see and follow the tracks. And, as daylight increased, he could run once more. He followed the trail down the mountain, and up the side of another one. Along its crest he went, down and up another mountain. And it was from the top of this that he heard a dog's bark.

Danny stopped, let his jaw drop open the better to listen. The bark was not repeated, but there had been no mistake about hearing it. Danny looked down into the wide, boulder-studded valley that stretched beneath him, and put his fingers into his mouth preparatory to whistling. But he stopped himself in time. If the bear and dog were down there, a whistle or sound would only warn Old Majesty that he was coming, and would send him off on another wild chase. Danny studied the valley carefully. The trees in it were only saplings and fire cherries, but the boulders were huge. The bear would make his stand against a boulder rather than one of the small trees. Danny scrutinized each boulder, and selected the one from which he thought the dog's bark had drifted.

But he had to go very carefully now, very slowly. A wrong move, a mis-step, and everything would be ruined. He walked down the mountain. Once on the valley floor he dropped to his hands and knees and crawled, placing each hand and foot carefully, cautious that his clothing should brush against no branch or twig that might make a sound. A hundred feet from the boulder he had chosen, he peered over a small rock and saw Old Majesty.

Perched on a shelf of rock, the bear was five feet from the ground. Huge, monstrous, a presence rather than a beast, his great head was bent toward the ground. Danny saw Red, lying on the ground ten feet before the bear, raising his head suspiciously every time the bear moved, ready to charge or retreat. Danny's hands trembled when he levelled his rifle over the little rock. This was a heaven-sent chance.

Ross had told him that a show dog must be no less than perfect, and there was one chance in fifty of killing that huge bear with a single shot. He would come toppling from his perch with snapping jaws and slashing paws. Red, knowing that at last he was reinforced by the man for whom he had waited, would be upon the bear. Not long, just long enough to get a ripped foot or a slashed side before Danny could send home the shot that would kill the bear. Just long enough to make him entirely useless to Mr. Haggin, to give Danny a chance of getting him. Danny sighted. Then he took his rifle down and crawled around the little rock.

He slithered over the ground, crawling forward with ready rifle held before him, and was twenty feet from the boulder when Old Majesty, all of whose attention had been riveted on the dog, looked up. The rank odor of the great bear filled Danny's nostrils, and for a moment he looked steadily into the eyes of his ancient enemy. Then Red was beside him, backing against Danny's knees, still looking at the bear. Danny's left hand reached down to grasp the dog's collar, his right brought the rifle up.

But Old Majesty slid off the back end of the boulder and was gone.

With the dog beside him, Danny started back up the mountain, but early twilight had come again when he and Red got back to Mr. Haggin's estate. Danny scarcely knew that his clothing was in tatters, that he was gaunt from lack of sleep and food. He knew only that he had brought Mr. Haggin's dog safely back. They went to the barn, and Robert Fraley came running from the house.

"Where have you had that dog?" he raged. "Half the estate's looking for him!"

He came close, Red backed against Danny's knees and growled. Robert Fraley pivoted, went to the barn and snatched a whip from its peg. He strode back to Danny and raised it.

"Don't hit that dog," Danny warned.

"Why, you . . ."

Danny lashed out with his right fist and smacked Robert Fraley squarely on the chin. The overseer fell backward, sat in the dust supporting himself on both hands, and blinked. Then he rose, and stepped back to clench his fists, when someone said,

"The war's over, Bob. You can go."

Danny turned slowly, and saw Mr. Haggin leaning against the barn. There were tears in Danny's eyes, and he was very much ashamed that anyone should see him cry. But he could do nothing else except kneel and put both arms around Red's neck.

"Nobody hits this dog where I can see it," he sobbed. "He, he's honest and clean, Mr. Haggin. He couldn't do a wrong thing, and nobody hits him for doin' right."

"Bob's a good man," Mr. Haggin was saying. "He'll see that things get done, and he has a lot of knowledge. But there are things he could learn about animals."

Danny stood erect and wiped the tears from his eyes. He was a man, and must act the part.

"I fetched your dog back, Mr. Haggin," he said. "He tracked that big bear to a standstill, the only dog with the heart to do it and the brain to handle the bear after he did. But I didn't shoot the bear, though I might have. You can still have a blue ribbon with Red. Feel him over yourself. Nothin's marred."

"No," Mr. Haggin said, but he was looking at Danny instead of the dog. "I guess nothing's marred. The dog isn't scratched and probably he might have been. Danny, how would you like to go to New York?"

Danny looked at Mr. Haggin, and for the first time saw him as something apart from the great Wintapi estate. He was a man, too, one who could love and understand a great dog, and see him as other than just a device for winning another blue ribbon. Somehow Danny knew that without having been there, Mr. Haggin knew just about what had happened in the Wintapi wilderness.

"With the dog," Mr. Haggin continued. "Bob Fraley's going to show him, and I'd like you to be along to sort of learn how it's done. Then I'd like to have you bring him back, and keep him at your house in the beech woods. He'll be the beginning of a long line of champions for the new kennels I'm planning and I believe you are the one to take charge of them. You see, I sort of like to have fine things around me, Danny, and I haven't time to take care of all of them myself."

"I couldn't do it," Danny said gravely. "Red, he's a

fightin' dog, Mr. Haggin. Mebbe I wouldn't allus be with him, and he might get clawed or chawed. Then he'd be good for no more shows."

Danny stood breathless, awaiting Mr. Haggin's certain agreement. But his eyes lighted up and a happy smile broke on his face when Mr. Haggin said, "Don't let that worry you, Danny. Take your dog up in the beech woods, and get yourself some sleep. Then come down, and I'll have Bob Fraley give you some pointers on what he's going to do."

CHAPTER 2

THE JOURNEY

THE SUN ROSE OVER STONEY LONESOME, AND HUNG LIKE a burning balloon in the sky as Danny danced back up the Smokey Creek trail. The savage, silent, head-swinging bear still roamed the Wintapi, an implacable, hating enemy of all the humans who trod there. But the bear was like the snows that piled up, the gales that roared through the forest, the occasional fire, all the things that those who lived in the Wintapi had to accept as a matter of course and deal with as best they could. The Wintapi could be a hard and lonely place.

But, hard as it might be, it would never again be lonely. Danny shook his whirling head, trying to arrange in some order the events that had brought about this miracle. He looked at the great red dog pacing beside him, and when he was safely screened by the forest knelt to pass both arms about Red's neck and hug him tightly. To be sure it was not his dog in the same sense that the mule, the hounds, and the four pigs were owned by his father. But as Red's caretaker he would naturally keep the dog with him; Mr. Haggin himself had said that.

Danny whirled into the clearing, waltzed with Red up the shanty steps, and burst through the door. Ross's rifle and belt of cartridges leaned beside it. A made-up pack lay on the table, and his father was lacing a pair of hiking moccasins on his bare feet.

"Pappy, I'm goin' to New York!" Danny bubbled happily.

"You're what?"

Danny sat breathlessly down on a chair. Red padded over, laid his head on Danny's knee, and turned his eyes to watch Ross, as though trying to fathom the welcome that he might expect from this other occupant of his new home. Outside, the four chained hounds whined uneasily and Asa sent an ear-splitting bray screaming across the pasture. Danny tickled Red's ear, and the big setter sighed happily. Starry-eyed, Danny stared at the shaft of sunlight streaming through the open door, and his feet seemed to be carrying him step by step back up it. He was jarred back to earth by Ross's gentle, "Speak sensible, boy."

"Yes, Pappy. I'm goin' to New York."

"That ain't sensible."

"But I am!" Danny insisted. "Mr. Haggin's sendin' Red down there to a show. That Fraley, he's takin' him and I'm goin' along to watch!"

"Sure, you're funnin' with me."

"I'm not. I was goin' to take Red back to Mr. Haggin. Instead, he lit out after that big bear that's been plaguin' us for so long. I had to find him. Red run that bear right to a standstill!"

"That dog run Ol' Majesty to a standstill?"

"Yes, sir."

"I hardly believe it," Ross breathed. "Go on, Danny."

"Red had the bear on a rock, way back in the pine valleys," Danny continued. "I could of shot, but didn't on account I knew the bear'd tumble off the rock and hurt the dog. So I caught up the dog and took him back to Mr. Haggin. That Fraley, he started a fuss. Then Mr. Haggin come. He said he could see the dog wasn't hurt. Then he told me that he was startin' a new kennel, and I was the one to take charge of it! First thing I got to do is go to New York and see Red in the dog show. Then I'm goin' to bring him back and we're goin' to keep him here."

Ross said, "That do beat all!"

He sat staring at the floor, but when he turned his eyes on Danny pride and pleasure lighted them. A wandering trapper most of his life, he had settled in the Wintapi twenty years ago. He knew his own handicaps and limitations, and since Danny was born he had striven desperately but hopelessly to give him some of the better things. Danny was not just a trapper. He was like his dead mother, with all her charm and intelligence. The pride in Ross's eyes increased. Quality, whether it was in a man or dog, just couldn't be hidden.

"Pappy," Danny asked seriously, "why do you think Mr. Haggin wants me to go?"

"I dunno, Danny. Mebbe he figures you're goin' to be a good enough dog man to handle his dogs at them big places."

Ross looked thoughtfully at his son. Danny had been a natural dog handler since babyhood, and if he could have an opportunity such as this . . . Ross had been around enough to know that people who handled rich men's dogs could make more money in a year than some trappers made in a lifetime. They could be somebody, too.

"Get some sleep, boy," Ross advised. "Your eyes are redder'n an old coon's that's been runnin' the cricks three nights straight."

"I'm not tired."

"Of course you're not. You ain't been up but two days and two nights. If you're goin' to New York with Red, you got to be ready. Lie down a bit of time."

"Well, mebbe a bit of time."

Danny lay down on his bed and Red curled up beside it. Danny's hand trailed over the side of the bed, feeling the big dog's furry back and assuring himself that it was really there. Ross put the yoke across his shoulders, hung his empty honey pails on it, closed the door softly behind him, and went into the woods.

Danny awoke with a start. The smell of frying pork chops tickled his nostrils. Red was sitting in the doorway, happy tail thumping the floor. Ross stood over the kitchen stove, turning pork chops in a skillet, and the long shades of evening were stealing across the clearing in the beech woods. Danny sprang out of bed, and looked at the windows.

"It's night!"

"Sure," Ross grinned. "For a man who wasn't tired, you did right well. That big red dog has been sittin' there watchin' me for the whole hour I been home. I think he would of bit me if I'd woke you."

Red trotted back to Danny, buried his muzzle in Danny's cupped hand, and sniffed. Danny looked away, and Red bumped his forehead gently against Danny's wrist, demanding more attention. Ross looked proudly from Danny to the dog, and his eyes drank in all the things that a born dog man will see in a fine dog.

"He's goin' to be the best varmint dog we ever had, Danny," he finally pronounced.

"Varmint dog?"

"Sure. You ain't just goin' to keep him in the house. That dog's got to hunt. It's born in him."

"I reckon you're right, Pappy."

Danny swung out of bed, crossed the floor to the two tin pails that stood on a wooden shelf, and poured a basin full of water. He washed his face and hands, and tried to bring from among the thoughts in his mind one that sought expression. But he could not quite find it. Red a varmint dog . . . Of course he would be a very good one, or he never could have bayed Old Majesty. A frown crossed Danny's brow, and he sat down to eat the fried potatoes and chops his father had prepared. Red caught a piece of meat tossed to him, and swallowed it daintily. Ross watched him.

"I'm right proud," he said, "to have a dog like that around. He's goin' to do a lot for us, Danny."

"I reckon he is."

"Yes, sir," Ross said profoundly. "We'll get more varmints this year than we ever had before. Is Mr. Haggin goin' to pay you anything for his keep?"

"Gee. I dunno."

"He needn't," Ross observed. "Such a dog will pay for his own keep, and ours too. By the way, one of Mr. Haggin's hired men was up here about two hours past. He wants you should bring the dog down, come mornin', so you can go to New York."

"He did? Then I guess we're really goin' after all, Pappy."

"You sure are. You'll see a heap of sights in New York, Danny. I come close to goin' there once, for a pelt man. But I couldn't abide in a city."

"I couldn't either."

"I know it, Danny. But you can go there sometimes

without hurtin' you. If you're finished, take your dog out and get him acquainted. I'll wash the dishes."

With Red trailing at his heels, Danny walked through the door into the evening twilight. The four chained hounds sulked beside their kennels. Old Mike, leader of the pack, raised his lips to disclose long fangs. Red trotted stiffly up, and Mike came stiffly forward. The two dogs sniffed noses and Mike, who knew a superior when he met one, sat down to watch with mournful eyes while Red nosed around an inviting patch of briers. A rabbit burst out of them, and went scooting toward the forest with Red in close pursuit. Forgetting their resentment, the four hounds bayed thunderous encouragement. The rabbit dived into a hole beneath a pile of rocks.

Danny watched critically. It was an amateurish exhibition in a way. Red had a good nose but lacked experience. Old Mike would have known that the rabbit was faster than he, and would have worked out a ruse to try and catch it by strategy. But Red was fast and smart. He would learn anything a dog could learn.

Danny took him over to the pasture. The black and white cow, feet braced and head extended, stared at this newcomer into the Pickett domain. The mule, customarily indifferent to everything except food, ignored Red and went right on cropping the short grass. Danny swung for a short walk in the woods, and when they returned to the shanty Ross was sitting at the table sharpening fish hooks. He looked up.

"How'd he do?"

"All right. He needs some smartin' up, but he'll do good."

"Sure he will. You best get some sleep."

Danny stifled a yawn, "I got up just four hours past."

"You could still sleep some more."

Danny folded an old quilt, and spread it on the floor near his bed. He took off his clothes and lay down, again letting his hand trail over the side of the bed and caress the big setter's back. He wasn't sleepy; a man who had slept from dawn to dark just couldn't be. Red sighed happily, and Danny wriggled on the bed. Slowly he faded into sound slumber, until he was awakened by the sound of Red's toenails clicking on the uncarpeted floor. The big dog padded to the door, then came back to rear on the bed and nudge Danny's shoulder with his muzzle. Danny rolled over and sat up. Bright sunlight streamed through the window. A chattering flicker's strident call rattled through the morning.

Danny swung out of bed, started a wood fire in the kitchen stove, and mixed pancake batter in a bowl. Ross stirred sleepily, and came into the kitchen to wash his face and hands in the tin basin. They ate breakfast, and Red expertly caught the bits of pancake Danny tossed to him. Danny picked up his fork, and drummed on the table's edge with its handle.

"You ever been to a dog show, Pappy?"

"Nope. Never have. But now that I'm older, it's often my wish that I had gone around to see more things when I was young. Whyfore you fidgetin', boy?"

"I dunno."

Ross grinned. "Put on your good clothes and pack your baggage. Then git on down to Mr. Haggin's. I'll take care of things here."

"I can't leave you with all the work!"

"Nine dishes to wash off," Ross scoffed. "Git goin'."

"Well, all right."

Danny donned his one presentable suit of clothes, painfully knotted a bright blue tie about his throat, and packed Ross's worn carpetbag. He stood stiffly before the door, with his hand on the knob, and Ross glanced at him with studied unconcern.

"I'll see you when you come back. Good luck, Danny."

Danny gulped, "Thanks, Pappy. I ain't afraid."

"I know you ain't. New York's goin' to seem a funny place. But just remember that a smart hound'll make out no matter where he hunts, given he keeps his nose to the wind. I'll rub a rabbit's foot for you."

"I'll try to do good. So long, Pappy."

"So long."

Danny walked out the door, and Red leaped happily up to pad beside him. A squirrel flashed across the trail, and Red sprang at it. The squirrel ascended a tree, and balanced saucily on a swaying branch while Red bounded on down the trail to overtake Danny. A buck snorted from a thicket, and farther down, near the border of the beech woods, some of Mr. Haggin's finely bred young calves raised their heads to stare. Danny broke into the edge of the clearing, and Red fell in beside him as both slowed to a sober walk. Mr. Haggin and Robert Fraley stood together near the barn. Danny came close, and stood without speaking while Red sat on the ground with his back against Danny's knees. Mr. Haggin turned to smile.

"Good morning, Danny."

"Mornin', sir."

"Turn the dog over to Bob, will you? I want to talk with you."

"Yes, sir."

Robert Fraley came forth with a short leather leash. Red backed closer to Danny's knees, and turned to look appealingly up. The overseer snapped the leash on Red's collar, forced him to mount a small wooden bench that stood against the barn, and snapped the other end of the leash into an iron ring. He entered the barn, to come out with a pair of clippers and a pair of shears. Danny looked questioningly at Mr. Haggin.

"He's only going to be trimmed," Mr. Haggin said. "We're leaving for New York at noon."

"Yes, sir, Pappy told me."

Mr. Haggin laughed. "He did, eh? Come on along, Danny."

His head turned slightly so he could see Red, Danny followed Mr. Haggin toward the barn door. Alert and erect, Red strained at the leash and kept his eyes on Danny. Then, just as Danny disappeared, the big red dog sighed and relaxed to let the familiar shears creep about his neck. Mr. Haggin entered a small office, sat down in a swivel chair, and motioned Danny into another one. He took a package of cigarettes from his pocket and extended them. Danny shook his head.

"No thanks. Pappy, he don't hold with either smokin' or drinkin'."

Mr. Haggin said thoughtfully, "The more I know of your father, the more I respect him." Then, "Danny, why do you suppose I turned Boy over to you, and am asking you to go to New York?"

"I don't rightly know."

"No, I don't suppose you do. But some wise man did a neat turn with an old axiom when he said that if a man is known by the company he keeps, a company is known by the men it keeps. Throughout my whole life I've seldom bet on anything but men, and I've seldom lost. I'm betting on you now."

"I don't know if I can do things for you, sir."

"That's my worry, Danny. I'm getting to the time of life when I can let others handle business affairs and devote my attention to the things I really like. One of those things is dogs, fine dogs. And I want you to help me. Five years from now I expect that you'll be taking my dogs, or rather our dogs, to shows and field trials all by yourself. What do you say, Danny?"

"I'll work very hard."

"I know you will, and you're going to have to work very hard. There are endless things you have to learn, and your education starts right now. I'm sending only Boy to this show, and Bob Fraley's in complete charge. You're going along to learn. Now I want to ask you a question; exactly what do you think of dog shows?"

"They seem like a piddlin' waste of time," Danny confessed.

"Danny, you're wrong. You would be entirely right if all a dog show amounted to was a bit of ribbon, or a cup, and a boost to the owner's pride. But there's more than that in it, much more. In one sense you could think of it as part of the story of man, and his constant striving toward something better. A dog show is illustrative of man's achievement, and a blue ribbon is more than a bit of silk. It's a mark, Danny, one that never can be erased. The dog that wins it will not die. If we send Boy to the show, and he comes back as best of breed, then that's something for all future dog lovers and dog owners to build on. Don't you see? A hundred years from now someone may stand on this very spot with a fine Irish setter, and he'll trace its lineage back to some other very fine setter, perhaps to Boy. And he will know that he has built on what competent men have declared to be the very best. He will know also that he, too, can go one step nearer the perfection that men must and will have in all things. It did not start with us, Danny, but with the first man who ever dreamed of an Irish setter. All we're trying to do is advance one step farther and Boy's ribbon, if he wins one, will simply be proof that we succeeded."

"I see," Danny breathed. "I never thought of it like that before."

"Always think of it that way, Danny," Mr. Haggin urged. "If you do, one day I'll see you as a leading dog handler. I'm sending Boy in the station wagon. I suppose you'd like to ride with him?"

"I'd sort of like to keep him company."

"I thought so," Mr. Haggin laughed. "When you come back at the end of the week I'll give you your first month's wages."

"Wages?"

"Yes, your beginning pay as a kennel man for me is fifty dollars a month. I'll increase that whenever you're worth an increase."

"Gee, Mr. Haggin, that's an awful lot!"

Mr. Haggin said crisply, "Suppose you go out and watch what Bob's doing. I'll see you in New York."

"Yes, sir."

Danny walked out of the barn, and stopped at the edge of the door to watch. Something was wrong on the wooden bench. Red was still there, and Robert Fraley was working over him with clippers and shears. But something that Danny had seen in the big dog was no longer there. Then a little wind played around the corner of the barn, and the illusion faded. Red's head lifted, he wagged his tail, and made a little lunge on the bench. Robert Fraley turned irritably around.

"Listen, kid, I've got orders to take you along. But I've also got orders that you're going only to watch. Don't stick your bill in unless it's asked for."

Danny said bluntly, "I ain't aimin' to bother you."

He sat quietly in the grass, watching the shears work smoothly around Red's throat. Golden-red hair came off in little wisps and bunches, and Robert Fraley retreated ten feet to stand critically inspecting his work. Danny looked from the handler to the dog. Red's throat was cleaner, straighter, and the fine curve of his neck a little more pronounced. His ears, trimmed, looked a little longer than they had and clung more tightly to his head. Danny said,

"You left a little raggedy patch, there just back of his right ear."

"I suppose you could do a better job?"

"I didn't say that. I just said you left his right ear raggedy."

"Well, I saw that myself, kid. And I told you before not to stick your bill in until it's wanted."

Robert Fraley finished trimming the ragged ear, and disappeared inside the barn. Danny stole forward to pick up a tin pail that was set under a dripping faucet, and gave Red a drink. The dog lapped thirstily, and Danny tickled his ear with one finger while he stared resentfully at the barn. That Fraley, he might know all about dog shows and such things, but he didn't even know enough about dogs to offer one a drink on a hot day. Danny put the pail back under the faucet, and retreated to his seat in the grass as Robert Fraley came out of the barn. A shining station wagon purred down from the house, and a uniformed chauffeur took a cigarette from his mouth to grin at Danny.

"You going, kid?"

"Yes, sir."

"Well, get in."

Danny said firmly, "I'll wait for the dog."

"Well, don't say you weren't invited."

Robert Fraley unsnapped Red's leash, led the big red setter to the station wagon, and permitted the leash to drag while Red climbed in to take his place in one of the back seats. Fraley sat down beside the chauffeur, and turned to look snappishly at Danny.

"Are you coming? Or shall I put a leash on you too?"

Danny said slowly, "You can try it if you're feelin' awful fit."

He squeezed past the front seat into the back, while the station wagon purred away from Mr. Haggin's Wintapi estate down to the black-top road leading to it. They went from that to macadam, and on for hour after hour while the rolling countryside swept past. Danny sat still, gazing through the window, raptly attentive to everything. He had never been out of the Wintapi, or more than forty miles from the shanty in the beech woods, and a man didn't really know what the world was until he got out to see it. They came to a city, but the station wagon rolled right through.

Late that evening they finally crossed the Pulaski Skyway. Red slept beside him, and Danny looked blankly at all the lights that seemed to be New York at night. They were everywhere, some low to the ground and some so high in the air that it was a wonder a man could climb that high to put in a light. Still puffing one of his innumerable cigarettes, the chauffeur turned around.

"That's the big place, kid."

"Yes, sir."

Red stirred, and lifted his head in the darkness to nudge Danny's hand. Danny pulled his ears, and swallowed the lump in his throat. This, exactly as Ross had said, was fine to see. But he seemed to be feeling the little breezes that played in the Wintapi at night, and hearing the night sounds that drifted out of the beech forests. He belonged there, along with Ross, Red, and everything else that was truly at home in the Wintapi. But he could still come to New York sometimes—provided Red came with him. The chauffeur threaded an expert way through the streets, weaving in and out of the traffic that clogged them, while Danny stared in wide-eyed wonder. The station wagon rolled to a stop before a big, lighted building and without speaking Robert Fraley got out to lead Red inside.

The chauffeur lit another cigarette, shielding the match with his hand, and leaned back to puff luxuriously. Danny stared anxiously at the building into which Robert Fraley had taken Red, and looked questioningly at the chauffeur.

"I got orders to deliver you to Haggin's town house, kid," the chauffeur said. "I hope that dog don't get hydrophobia and bite Fraley. If he does, Fraley's sure going to bite you."

"He don't like me," Danny said gravely. "I hit him in the chin."

"You did?" the chauffeur grinned. "I always miss the nicest things that happen."

"Are we comin' back here?" Danny asked anxiously.

"Oh, sure. Haggin'll bring you back; he wants you to see the show. Don't worry about your goulash hound."

"It's a setter," Danny corrected.

"Well, don't worry about your setter then. Let's go." Again the station wagon purred into life, and the chauffeur wove his way through crowded streets to a house that was one of a row of brown-stone houses. He got out, and Danny followed with his carpetbag while the chauffeur ascended a flight of stone steps, guarded by stone lions, and pressed a button. The door opened, and a butler stood framed in the light.

"Hi, Bill," the chauffeur remarked cheerfully, "I'm back from the wilds with a wild man. Haggin said turn him over to you."

The butler said primly, "Mr. Haggin has not yet arrived, but I shall be happy to care for you, sir. Will you please follow me?"

He reached down for Danny's bag, but Danny grinned and picked it up.

"I can carry my own parcels."

He followed the butler through a hall, and up a flight of polished stone steps into a room. Danny put his bag down and stared. The room, with a canopied bed in the center, was half as big as the shanty where he and Ross lived in the beech woods.

"Will you have dinner in your room, sir?" the butler asked.

Danny gulped. All this for him seemed hardly real or right. But he was hungry. A little pang assailed him. Neither he nor Red had eaten since morning, and Red was probably hungry too. Danny smiled at the butler.

"I'd take it right kindly if you brought me some vittles, sir."

The butler smiled back, and his stiff formality seemed to leave him. He winked at Danny.

"I'll bring you some. Go ahead and wash up. What would you like to eat?"

"Uh . . . Uh . . . Pork chops are always good."

The butler left and Danny entered the bathroom to wash his face and hands in the porcelain basin. For a long while he stood pleasurably watching the cold water run out of the faucet. His mother, whom he could remember only dimly, had never had such marvels to serve her, and he and Ross got their water from a pump. But the beech woods was still a good place, and a man couldn't rightly expect to have everything. He dried his face, combed his wet hair, and re-entered the bedroom to find a table set and chair ready. He ate hungrily, gnawing the last shreds of meat from the pork chops and crunching the last of a small mountain of French fried potatoes. He would, he guessed, have to learn to make such potatoes himself so Ross could enjoy them too. For a few minutes he sat idly looking out of the window, until the butler came to take the table away.

Danny took off his clothes and lay down on the luxurious bed. The room seemed to whirl about. Red was looking anxiously at him, pleading with soft eyes and gently wagging tail. Danny turned over, and closed his eyes to shut the vision out. But he couldn't. He sat up in the darkness, resting against the bed's head-board. All he knew was that, if Red was suddenly taken away from him, neither he nor Red could be happy again. That Fraley, who understood the fine points of dog shows without coming even close to understanding dogs . . .

Danny shivered, and slid back down into the bed.

CHAPTER 3

THE DOG SHOW

ALL NIGHT HE LAY ON THE SOFT BED, SOMETIMES DROP-
ping into a fitful doze but for the most part staring at the
dark ceiling. Occasionally his thoughts turned to Ross,
and the shanty in the beech woods, and at such times
Danny moved restlessly. Probably Ross would know
exactly what to do, and how to go about doing it, but the
only parting advice he had given Danny was that a

smart hound could hunt anywhere if he kept his nose into the wind. Danny squirmed, and tried to quiet the thoughts that tormented him. Mr. Haggin must have known what he was doing when he appointed Robert Fraley to show the dog. Just the same . . .

Danny remembered vividly the trimming bench in the Wintapi. Red had been under Fraley's hands then, and he had been only an animated statue instead of a dog. The wonderful thing that lived in Red, and made him what he was, just didn't show when Fraley was handling him. The first gray streaks of dawn stole through the windows, and outside the quiet street came to life. Danny dropped into a dream-troubled sleep.

He was awakened by the sound of music, playing through a loud-speaker in the wall, and sprang up in bed. For a moment he rubbed his eyes, and looked bewilderedly about the room in which he found himself. Some of the notes coming from the radio were almost exactly like those of the bell-throated thrush that used to sing outside his window when early dawn came to the Wintapi. He oriented himself and swung his bare feet to the floor. This wasn't the Wintapi. It was New York. Red was here to win a blue ribbon so that for all time to come sportsmen who loved dogs would know how fine he was. Danny was here, if for nothing else, to cheer while he won it. He entered the bathroom, washed, and was knotting the blue tie about a clean shirt he had taken out of the carpetbag when someone knocked softly on the door. It opened a crack, and Mr. Haggin called cheerfully,

"Good morning, Danny. How goes it? Sleep well?"

"Fine, sir."

Mr. Haggin entered the room and sat down on the edge of the bed. He lit a cigarette, puffed twice on it, and pinched it out. His shoe beat a nervous little tattoo on the floor. Danny looked at him, and away again. Mr. Haggin, obviously bothered by something, rose to pace around the room and again sit down on the edge of the bed.

"How do you like New York?" he asked.

"I haven't seen much of it."

Mr. Haggin laughed. "A good enough answer." For a moment he was silent. Then he said, "Danny, Boy's going up today. And, let me tell you, he's going to fight for any wins he makes. The best Irishmen in the country, and some from other countries, are here. But, Danny, if Boy can win his three points today, we'll have a champion!"

Danny knitted a puzzled brow, "I thought he was that before."

"No," Mr. Haggin admitted. "I always called him champion, and thought of him as such, but he isn't written as champion into the records of the American Kennel Club. You see, according to the competition he meets, a dog can win points at every show. He has to win two three-point shows under different judges, and nine other points, before he is officially a champion. Boy has his nine points, and one three-point show. He *can* win five points at this show. He's *got* to win three!"

"How are such things rated?" Danny asked.

"By the general excellence of the dog. A judge will examine his head, eyes, ears, neck, body, shoulders and forelegs, hind legs, tail, coat and feathering, color, size, style, and general appearance, and rate him accordingly. If two dogs are equal physically, the one with the most 'dog personality' will win. I want you to watch the judge, and the handlers with their dogs, and ask me any questions you care to while the judging is in progress. You'll learn that way. Danny, Boy's as good as any Irish setter in the show!"

"I know that, sir."

Mr. Haggin was looking at him, and Danny felt strangely drawn to the older man. They were not a wealthy dog fancier and his apprentice handler, but two men who could be brought very close by a common bond—the love of a good dog. Danny licked his dry lips. You could get all the best dogs from all over, and have every hair in place on every one of them, and if they were all exactly alike two or three would still stand out and one would stand out from those. That thing Mr. Haggin had referred to as dog personality . . . Maybe every dog had it, but had no reason for revealing it.

"Do you s'pose we can see Red before the show?" Danny asked.

Mr. Haggin coughed nervously and looked away. "I'm afraid not. Bob always likes to handle a dog without interference, especially on a show day. You can see him right after the show."

"Yes, sir."

"Come on down and have some breakfast," Mr. Haggin urged. "We'll both feel better. Doggonit, Danny, I'm as nervous as a sixteen-year-old going sparking for the first time."

They ate, and Mr. Haggin retreated to an inner office to conduct some business of his own while Danny roamed about the house. Pictures of horses and dogs lined the walls of one big room, and on the mantelpiece Danny found a small folder containing one worn snapshot. It was of a fifteen-year-old boy, with bare feet thrust out of tattered overalls, and a cane pole in one hand and a string of sunfish in the other. Danny peered closely at it, and held it up to the light. When he replaced it on the mantel he knew that it was a boyhood picture of Mr. Haggin. The lord of this luxurious manor and the great Wintapi estate had not, then, always been wealthy.

Danny sat down on a sofa, looking about at the books, the pictures, the trophies, all the things that throughout the years Mr. Haggin had gathered. He leaned back to close his eyes, and thought curiously that he was no longer the same person who had come out of the Wintapi. He had learned, and with added knowledge seemed to have grown. He thought of Red, and his eyes glowed. Back in the Wintapi, no matter what it looked like, a dog was esteemed according to its hunting ability. But to have a dog with hunting ability, and all the brains, the courage, and the heart that a dog like Red had too! If such dogs came about as a result of competitive dog shows, then certainly only a fool would scoff at or belittle them.

Danny's eyes clouded, and again he seemed to see Red beside him, in trouble and needing help. He rose to pace about the room, peering into wall cases at Mr. Haggin's books and trophies. If only he was back in the Wintapi he would know exactly what to do and nobody could tell him that he was just an onlooker. Danny clenched and unclenched his hand. Try as he would to please Mr. Haggin, he could not feel like just an onlooker here either. Red had something great at stake, and Danny must help him triumph.

It was an eternity before the butler came in to announce lunch. Mr. Haggin was more composed, but an excited little light that he could not control still danced in back of his eyes. Danny ate broiled steak, mashed potatoes, asparagus, and a wonderful kind of pudding that floated in whipped cream. He made a mental note to inquire about that kind of pudding, so he could make some for Ross when he got back to the Wintapi. He looked up as Mr. Haggin started to speak.

"As I've already told you, Danny, the basic idea of a dog show is to determine the best dogs. It's really an elimination contest, with the inferior dogs being weeded out and the best ones winning the awards. Naturally you can't take seventy-five dogs, throw them all together, and pick out the best. So the dogs are divided into classes. The puppy class is open to any qualified dog more than six months and less than one year old. No imported dog, except those from Canada, may be entered in that class. The novice class is open to any dog that has not won a first prize at an American Kennel

Club show, and a surprise winner often comes from it. The limit class is open to any dog except A.K.C. champions, and imported dogs may enter it. The winner's class, of course, determines the best of winners. As a general rule, in all of these classes, dogs and bitches are judged separately. Do you know why?"

"I think so," Danny answered gravely. "They aren't alike. A dog wants to be big, strong, and husky, same's a man. A bitch can be strong but . . . There's the same difference between them as there is between a woman and man. It would be hard to judge them together."

"That's right," Mr. Haggin nodded approvingly. "Although of course the winner's dog competes with winner's bitch for best of breed. But there's another class, the open, and Boy's entered in that. The open's where you usually find the hottest competition, and it's certainly here this time. Imported dogs may enter it, and Art Maugin came from London with Heatherbloom." Mr. Haggin closed his eyes. "Wait until you see Heatherbloom, Danny. He moves like a flame, and except for Boy is the finest Irish setter I've ever seen. Are there any questions you'd like to ask?"

"I can't rightly think of any," Danny admitted. "Probably I will after I've seen the show."

"Then let's go. Every man has a right to his own private superstitions, and I'd like to go in just as Boy's going into the ring. He needs luck, and we should time it just about right if we leave now."

They went out the front door, and entered a sleek, black limousine that awaited there. The chauffeur drove off, while Mr. Haggin relaxed in the back seat with closed eyes. Danny looked out of the window, eagerly drinking in all the things that were New York by day. He missed nothing from the blue-uniformed policemen at intersections to the newsboys who scooted along the sidewalks. The chauffeur stopped suddenly, and Danny looked ahead to see a uniformed officer directing traffic down a side street. Bright red fire trucks were huddled on the street from which they had been shunted, and smoke rolled from the fourth story of a building there. Mr. Haggin muttered to himself and looked at his watch. Finally the car rolled to a stop before the big building —Danny recognized it even by daylight—into which Robert Fraley had taken Red. He gulped, and tried to quiet the frightened little butterflies that were in his stomach. It was a huge building, big as all the buildings in the Wintapi, including Mr. Haggin's barns, and he didn't even know his way into it.

He got out with Mr. Haggin, and the chauffeur drove away down the street while they joined one of the lines of people moving through the doors. From somewhere Danny faintly heard the frenzied barking of a dog that was either excited or in distress. He listened attentively. But it wasn't Red. Close behind Mr. Haggin, he passed down an aisle to take his seat directly before one of two dog rings. Almost as soon as he sat down, he saw Red.

The dog had a short leather leash about his neck and was walking, to the left of Robert Fraley, around the ring. Danny skipped the thirteen dogs whose handlers were also gaiting them for the judge, and fastened his eyes on Red. His finger nails bit deeply into the palms of his hands, and his knuckles whitened. It had happened—exactly what he had feared most. The dog in the ring was not the one that had come wagging up to greet him, the dog of the Wintapi. He was not the Red Danny knew, but only an animated plaything that walked around the ring because he had been taught to do so. Beads of sweat gathered on Danny's brow.

A tiny piece of paper, borne by a gentle wind current, whirled over the ring and settled on the floor of the amphitheater twenty feet beyond it. Three of the dogs looked at it, but Red did not. Danny tore his eyes away from his idol to look at the other dogs.

He swallowed hard. Never before had he seen so many magnificent dogs—unless he had seen them it would be hard to believe that there were that many. His eyes skipped over two whose feet turned out slightly at the pastern, and whose gait was in a very slight degree erratic as compared to Red and the rest of the setters in the ring. He looked sideways at Mr. Haggin, and tried to keep from looking back into the ring. But he couldn't. His eyes were arrested by the third dog behind Red.

A rich, golden chestnut, with a narrow white blaze down his face, the dog at first glance seemed almost as magnificent as Red. He was big, with a long neck and a lean head. His front legs were very straight and strong, with beautifully symmetrical feathering flowing from them as he walked. His feet were tight, strong, and small, his chest deep with ribs well-spread for lung space. Long loins had a nice tuck-up before strong rear legs. His tail, extending slightly downward, waved gently as he walked.

Danny nudged Mr. Haggin and whispered, "Is that third one behind Red Heatherbloom?"

"It is," Mr. Haggin said. "I told you he was magnificent."

"He sure is," Danny breathed.

Another wisp of paper blew across the amphitheater as the dogs were lined up, head to tail, before the judge. Danny saw the judge confer with the two handlers whose dogs turned out at the pastern, and one of them led his dog around the ring again. Then both withdrew their entries. Danny looked approvingly at the judge. Such a defect wasn't easy to see, but if a show was to determine a dog's perfection then it was right that these two be withdrawn. The judge knelt beside the first dog in the row, and opened its mouth. Danny saw white teeth flash, and thought he saw the lower jaw protruding slightly ahead of the upper. He whispered to Mr. Haggin,

"That dog looks undershot."

Mr. Haggin grinned. "Maybe I should ask you questions. Where'd you learn the A.K.C. rules, Danny?"

"I didn't. But a body knows what's the matter with a dog. Fifteen dollars is a right smart heap of money to spend for a hound if you get one that can't run, or bite, or has no wind. A body's got to look for things in a dog."

The judge ran his hands over the dog's head and ears, on down the neck, and over the chest while the handler knelt at the rear, pulling gently on the tail. The judge moved to the rear, and the handler stepped quickly in front of the dog to grasp its head firmly and extend it.

"He's showing the neck-line," Mr. Haggin explained, "and steadying the dog."

The judge returned to the front, picked the dog up under the chest, and dropped him easily to the floor. Then he moved to the next dog, while the handler knelt before the one that had already been examined and stroked his charge. The judge went on down the line, and Danny watched wildly as he bent over Red. The big dog posed perfectly. His front legs and feet were set perpendicular on the floor, and from the hock down, his rear legs were also perpendicular. His neck stretched up and forward, his head and muzzle were level and parallel with the floor, and his tail sloped gently downward. But there was still something missing, something that should be there and was not.

The judge finished the last dog, and at a little trot the first handler ran his dog around the ring. He stopped, and again the judge knelt to examine the dog's jaws. The handler led his dog back to the bench, and one by one the rest of the handlers gaited their dogs.

Danny leaned excitedly forward. Heatherbloom, Red, and two dogs that Danny could not identify were up for the final judging. Mr. Haggin had said that Red needed luck. Danny crossed his fingers, but when he looked over his left shoulder to spit, he looked directly into the eyes of a fat and perspiring man behind him. Danny flushed, and swung around to watch while beads of perspiration gathered on his forehead. These four dogs were the best of all that had been entered in the open class. But the best of the four . . .

Danny stared beseechingly at Red, still an animated and beautiful statue under the expert hands of Robert Fraley. Heatherbloom lifted his head to look imperiously at the judge, and sweep the spectators with a commanding eye. Danny sucked in his breath, and once more his fingers bit deeply into the palms of his hands. The dog from England was alive, alert, challenging everyone to dare do anything but give him the blue ribbon. But he was still not so alive and alert as Danny had seen Red. Danny gripped the front of his seat, as though the very intensity of his will and thought would carry to Red the message that Danny wanted him to have. The judge leaned over Red, and passed on to Heatherbloom.

Danny said suddenly, "I'll be back, sir."

He arose and ran along the narrow corridor before the seats while people stared curiously at him and an usher made as if to stop him. Danny ran on, unheeding and uncaring. Finally he stopped in an aisle to stand and stare breathlessly back toward the ring. And he saw a miracle.

Red came suddenly alive. Physically he was the dog that Robert Fraley had led into the ring. But there was something about him now that had not been there before. Red was once more the dog of the Wintapi, the glorious dog that Danny had first seen when he went down to report to Mr. Haggin that the outlaw bear had killed another of his bulls. Danny saw the judge smile, and hand the blue winner's ribbon to Robert Fraley.

For a while Danny stood very still, watching the happy dog in the ring strain toward him. Ross had said that a smart hound could hunt anywhere if he kept his nose into the wind. And Ross was right. The pieces of paper, blowing across the amphitheater, had shown Danny which way the wind was blowing. All he had had to do was go stand in the wind current, and let his scent be carried by it, to prove to the dog that the boy he worshipped most was still standing by.

CHAPTER 4

DANNY'S HUMILIATION

FOR THREE HAPPY DAYS DANNY WANDERED ABOUT THE amphitheater, whenever Robert Fraley was absent, stopping at Red's bench, and when Fraley was present drifting about to study with fascinated eyes the many marvels that offered.

He saw dogs the like of which he had never dreamed before: mosquito-like little Chihuahuas, three of which

would not equal the weight of one big Wintapi snowshoe rabbit; lumbering St. Bernards, good-natured
beasts that might have swallowed the Chihuahuas
whole; stately Irish wolfhounds, that he studied carefully with a view to getting one for hunting bears; clean-
limbed hounds that shamed his father's varmint dogs;
greyhounds, made of whipcord and steel; collies too
beautiful for words, dachshunds, beagles, poodles, bas-
sets, spaniels, and from each he learned a little more of
the fascinating story of dogdom. He saw Red go up to
compete with the winning Irish setters of all classes and
get the purple ribbon for the best of dogs. Then he
watched him compete with the winning bitch, a viva-
cious little vixen of a setter almost as perfect as himself,
and win the blue and white ribbon of the best of breed.
Danny was present when Red missed by a hairsbreadth
being the best in show, and started happily home with
Mr. Haggin to dream of the great days through which
he had lived. Red hadn't won all the honors, but he had
won enough. He was an official champion.

Danny relaxed in the back seat of Mr. Haggin's
limousine, watching New York. It was a fascinating new
world, and one that he must see again. When he had
learned enough to handle Mr. Haggin's dogs at these
shows . . . The picture faded slowly, and in its place
Danny saw Smokey Creek, above the bridge where it
purled black against the beech roots and carved out
deep little recesses in which the trout hid. He saw the
last rays of the setting sun painting Stoney Lonesome
bright gold, and thought of thunderheads gathering

over Smokey Mountain. New York was right nice, but the job he had come there to help do was done and there was another waiting back in the Wintapi. Ross would be planning his trap-lines, and needed help. Red, who certainly was going to be a hunter as well as a show dog, would have to be getting into the beech woods and learning more about the ways of the various creatures that lived there.

Danny leaned a little farther back in the seat, suddenly anxious. Mr. Haggin folded the newspaper he had been reading and laid it on the seat beside him. For a moment they rode in silence. Then Mr. Haggin said a little wearily,

"The show's over, Danny, and we did what we set out to do."

"Yes, sir."

"Boy's an official champion now."

"Yes, sir."

Mr. Haggin looked curiously at him. "What's the matter, Danny?"

"I was thinkin'," Danny said bluntly. "That little bitch that went up with Red for best of winners, she was just a mite too close in the ribs and short in lung space. But you know what? If we ever had a bitch as good as that, and Red, the get of two such dogs . . ." Danny paused as though it was hard to imagine such a thing. "The get of two such dogs would be almost sure to have another pup as good as Red. Maybe better."

Mr. Haggin said, "There isn't enough money to buy that bitch from Dr. Dan MacGruder."

"I was only thinkin', sir," Danny sighed wistfully.

They rode in silence for a few more blocks, while Mr. Haggin stared out of the window. He had set his heart on Red's being best of breed, and winning that had been so important that it supplanted everything else. Then Red had won, and after glorying in that triumph Mr. Haggin, like Danny, was thinking of better dogs and better things.

"How far is it to the Wintapi?" Danny asked suddenly.

"About three hundred miles."

"Oh," said Danny. "I didn't think . . ."

"Of course," Mr. Haggin said easily, "Bob will want to stay here a few days to do the town, and maybe we won't go back for another week. Naturally you can stay if you want to. But I've been thinking that a newly made champion like Boy needs a lot of space to run around, and get in shape for his next show. So if you want to take him home by train tonight, I can give you your first month's wages and you can both go."

"You mean right away?"

"Strictly a business proposition," Mr. Haggin assured him. "And I'm glad that you see eye to eye with me on it. The first job of a dog handler is to look after his dog."

"I'll look after Red!" Danny breathed. "He'll get the best of care and mindin'. Do you think I could make him into a huntin' dog?"

"Of course. I think it'd be good for him. But you understand now why it's very important for him not to be disfigured."

Danny's face was troubled. "I already told you that, if you got him in the Wintapi, he might meet a varmint and get chewed or clawed."

"I understand that, Danny, and am willing to take the chance. But I don't want it to happen unnecessarily. I'll be seeing him around, of course, while I'm still in the Wintapi. After I leave I'll expect a monthly report from you."

"I can just as easy report every day."

"That won't be necessary." Mr. Haggin's eyes twinkled. He spoke softly to the chauffeur, and the big car drew up before a lighted drug store. Mr. Haggin entered the store, and when he came back the chauffeur took a circuitous route home. They got out, and Mr. Haggin rang the bell. There was a moment's pause, a scuffling inside, and as soon as the door was opened Red flung himself into Danny's arms. The flushed and apologetic butler stood just inside the door.

"The dog arrived only a few minutes ago," he explained. "I just could not control him."

"That's all right."

Mr. Haggin entered the house. The ecstatic Red, keeping as close to Danny as he could get, padded over the floor and every few seconds flung his head up to lick Danny's hands. He threw himself down by Danny's chair, stretched out his head, and sighed contentedly as the two ate dinner. Danny finished eating, then spoke hesitatingly.

"If there's any way you want to check up on how I'm takin' care of him . . ."

Mr. Haggin looked at Danny, and at the happy dog. "I've already checked," he said. He looked at his watch. "I don't want to hurry you, Danny, but you can get a train in half an hour."

"Yes, sir. I'm ready."

"Leave your bag here and I'll bring it through with me. You won't be needing it, will you?"

"No, sir," Danny smiled. "Not in the Wintapi."

"All right. Let's go."

Red climbed into the car and got up on the seat to lay his head on Danny's lap as they drove down to the station. Mr. Haggin bought tickets, and pressed them and a small roll of bills into Danny's hand.

"Here are your tickets and the rest of your first month's wages," he said. "I'll arrange for Boy."

He entered an office, telephoned, and came out to stand beside Danny and Red. A trainman followed him.

Mr. Haggin turned to Danny.

"I've arranged for Red to go in the baggage car," he said. "Be sure to get him out at the Wintapi station."

"Can't I go in the baggage car too?"

"You won't get any sleep," Mr. Haggin objected.

"I can sleep in the darndest places! Honest! Can't we ride together? Red might . . . might bite the baggage man and then you'd be in an awful fix!"

"Well . . . " Mr. Haggin looked at the trainman, who grinned and said, "C'mon." They passed through a gate, and the trainman spoke to the guard in the baggage car. He turned to wave his hand.

"You can both go. Hoist the pooch in."

Danny cradled Red in his arms and lifted him through the open door. The big dog stood peering back with tongue lolling and tail gently wagging while he watched Danny. Danny shook hands with Mr. Haggin.

"I want to thank you for everything," he said awkwardly.

Mr. Haggin laughed. "Think about the things you've seen and learned, Danny."

"I am thinkin' about such things."

"All right. See you in the Wintapi. Good luck."

"Good luck."

Danny climbed into the car and the guard rolled the door shut. He looked admiringly at Red.

"Your dog, kid?"

"No, sir. I'm only takin' care of him for Mr. Haggin."

"Hm-m," the guard grinned. "Haggin's got you under his wing, huh? If he didn't have, you never would have brought an uncrated dog into this car or ridden here as passenger yourself. But I guess owning half a railroad makes a difference in what you can do. Well, make yourselves at home."

Danny sat on a wooden crate, swinging his long legs from it while Red curled up beside him and slept. The train started, and only the noise of wheels on rails penetrated the baggage car. After a bit Danny got down from the crate, pillowed his head against it, and dozed. The guard tossed him a blanket.

"This may be softer."

Danny folded the blanket under his head, and Red crouched close beside him as the train rumbled through the night. At various times it stopped, and Red growled softly when the door was opened to receive more baggage. Danny awoke, sat up, and lay down again to pillow his head on the blanket. The lights in the car grew pale as slow dawn crept out of the sky. Danny rose, and with Red padding beside him looked about the car. Half asleep in a chair, the guard stirred and grinned.

"An hour more, kid. I'm going through to Morrisville myself, then back to the city. Do you live around these parts?"

"In the beech woods in the Wintapi," Danny said courteously. "My pappy and I, we're trappers there. Of course, now I'm goin' to be takin' care of Mr. Haggin's dog, too."

"I've hunted in the Wintapi," the guard said wistfully. "Once, when we laid over two days at Morrisville, I went to a place called Chestnut Creek and hunted deer. I didn't get any, but the man with me shot a big ten-pointer."

"Come up this season and I'll show you deer," Danny invited. "Ask at Mr. Haggin's place, and they'll tell you where Ross and Danny Pickett live."

"I might do just that. Let's get a little fresh air."

He opened the door, and Danny sat on a box to watch. They were in the hills, and the little farms that huddled close to their bases still slept in the gray dawn. Then they rounded a bend and, far off, he saw Smokey Mountain towering above all the rest. The train started slowing for the Wintapi station, and Danny stood eagerly erect.

When the train lurched to a stop, he jumped. He turned to help Red, but the big Irish setter had already leaped to the cinders beside him.

"So long," the guard yelled.

"So long."

Danny turned to wave, then started for the beech woods that began where the railroad's property ended. A mighty, leaping happiness coursed through him. The fuss and glamor of the dog show were done with. Mr. Haggin had the ribbons. But Danny had the dog. And now they were home, here in the Wintapi.

Red paced sedately beside him. But once in the woods, screened by trees from prying eyes that might see and comment on any let-down in dignity, Danny broke into a wild run. It seemed an eternity since he had seen the rough shanty where he and his father lived, smelled the good scent of streams, forests, and mountains, or had any part at all in the only life he had ever loved. With the dog racing beside him, Danny climbed over the jutting nose of a mountain, trotted up a long valley, climbed the ridge at its head, and descended the other side. He ran in almost a perfectly straight line to his father's clearing. Coming to the edge of it, Danny slowed to a walk. He knew by the smokeless chimney that his father wasn't home. Ross Pickett, naturally, would have been up at dawn and out scouting the ridges on a fine day like this.

But his father's four hounds strained at the ends of their chains and bayed a vociferous welcome. Danny grinned at them, and watched Red go up to renew acquaintance with Old Mike. The two dogs wagged stiff tails, and Mike sat down to blink indifferently at Danny.

Danny chuckled, and tickled the old hound's tattered ears while the three pups begged for attention. Red sat with his head cocked to one side and watched jealously. Danny stooped and unsnapped the chains. Wild to be free, the four hounds went in a mad race across the fields. They came tearing back and were away again. Red raced with them, but wheeled and came back when Danny whistled. Danny scratched his silken ears.

"Leave 'em go," he said. "Leave 'em go, Red. They'll just run awhile and come back. But you ain't goin' to run with ordinary hounds. You got more important work to do—given Pappy can think alike with me."

Red walked beside him when Danny went into the house. Outside, everything had been warm sunshine. But inside, where only glancing sunbeams strayed through the single-paned windows that Ross Pickett had set in the walls of his shanty, a definite chill prevailed. Danny stuffed tinder into the stove, lighted it, and added wood when it was blazing. He pulled aside the burlap curtain that hung over the cupboard, and took out a pot and skillet. Red trotted beside him when he went to the spring house for a piece of pork that Ross had left there to cool, and returned to lie in the center of the floor while Danny cooked the meat.

An hour later Red got up and went to sit before the door. There was a little pause, a heavy tread on the porch, and Ross Pickett came in.

"Danny!" he exclaimed. "I knowed you was home on account I heerd the hounds a-bayin'."

"Hello, Pappy. It sure is good to be home. You aimed to start out and scout a trap line?"

"Yup. Stoney Lonesome ridge for foxes. Ought to be a nice take of pelts this year. They's lots of rabbits for pelt animals to eat off."

But the shine in Ross's eyes belied the workaday talk, and the flutter in Danny's chest was far too intense ever to be put into words. He and his father had been so close for so long that they felt, and acted, and almost thought alike. Each was lost without the other, and now that they were together they could be happy again. Danny said with affected carelessness that could not hide the enormous pride he felt,

"I fetched the red dog home. There he is."

"Well, so you did!" Ross whirled about as though he had just noticed the magnificent setter. "That is a dog, Danny. I reckon you'n him must of cut some swath in New York, huh?"

"Red did in the dog ring. He got some prizes for Mr. Haggin."

"What you see in New York, Danny?"

"Dogs, little mites of dogs that Sanders Cahoon could tie on that watch chain he carries. Dogs most as big as a Shetland pony. Hounds that could course up Wintapi ravines. Dogs made to run so fast they could catch a fox . . ."

For two hours he talked on, explaining in minutest detail all the marvels to be encountered at a dog show, while Ross listened raptly. Red pushed the screen door open with his nose, and went outside to sit on the sun-drenched porch. A hawk, circling over the clearing, gave vent to a shrieking whistle and Red growled warningly at it. Then Ross looked at the tarnished dollar watch that he kept stuffed into the pocket of his blue overalls.

"That was mighty good talk," he sighed. "We'll have to talk some more when evenin' comes. But right now I got to horse myself up Stoney Lonesome. Given we don't have our fox sets staked out, we won't take many foxes."

"Shall I come along?" Danny asked.

"Nope, you stay here and watch that big dog. He ain't no woods dog yet, even though he did run Ol' Majesty to a standstill. He's got to get more used to the woods. When he does—by gummy, we can pull all our traps and take our pelts with him alone."

"Pappy, I think . . ." Danny hesitated.

"Speak your mind, boy," Ross urged.

"I think there's more ways of teachin' dogs to hunt than the ways we been usin'. I'd sort of like to try some of those ways on Red."

"Sure. He's your dog. Teach him any way you see fit. Well, I got to be off."

Ross went out the door, and Danny watched with miserable eyes while he tramped across the clearing and disappeared in the woods. Ross was counting on making a varmint dog of Red. There were just some things that Ross did not understand, but might understand if given the chance. Any mongrel with four legs and the ability to run could hunt varmints. Danny looked fondly at the big setter. The first man who had dreamed of an Irish setter had dreamed of a dog to hunt birds, and to make Red a varmint dog would almost be betrayal of that man and all the others who had striven to make the breed what it was.

With Red padding close beside him, Danny went down to the creek and a short way up it. Brook trout darted toward hidden crevices under the bank, and fat suckers lay inert in some of the deeper pools. Red stayed close behind Danny, going where he went and almost stepping in his tracks. After a bit he ranged out a little more, and when a chipmunk scurried across their path he dashed at it.

For four days they wandered around in the woods, never getting very far from the shanty, while Red slowly learned the true ways of the life that from now on was to be his. Danny watched him critically. Ruffed grouse, known throughout the Wintapi as partridges, were the only game birds in the section. A dog that would hunt them must at all times be under close control of the man with the gun. And Red, now that he was learning all about the fascinating things in the woods, gave no sign that he understood in the slightest degree any sort of control that a hunter's dog must have. Danny thought of a choke collar and check cord, and discarded the notion. There were other ways, and a dog that learned of its own free will always learned better than one that was forced.

The sun continued to shine through lazy summer days, and every day Ross was off to the hills or to some creek to determine where the most fur-bearers were running. Red and Danny prowled through the woods near the cabin. Then one morning, while Danny was sprawled across the porch with his straw hat over his eyes and Red lay curled near him, Ross came around the corner of the shanty.

"My gosh, Danny! I never in my life saw anything more do-less."

Danny sat up to grin. Red rose, padded down the steps to greet Ross, and came back to Danny. Ross shifted the two fishing rods he carried from his left hand to his right, and raised his head to stare at two black crows that were winging their raucous way across the valley.

"Trappin' season's just around the corner," he observed. "And by gummy, summer's the time to make ready to take furs when winter gets here."

Danny sat up a little straighter. "That's right." He looked at the fishing rods. "You goin' to catch shiners for bait?"

"That's what I'm goin' to do? Want to help?"

"I reckon. We ain't had a sashay since I went to New York."

"You been too busy with that big dog," Ross grunted. "How's he comin' on?"

"Good."

Danny rose and descended the steps, and Red padded after him. He held out his hand for one of the rods Ross carried, and a can of bait. Asa and the white and black cow raised their heads as the trio set off across the pasture. At the far end Danny stopped, and parted the wires so Red could get through. They left the sun-warmed clearing, entered the sunless and cooler beech woods, and Danny paused to watch a gray squirrel on the end of a mossy log. He had seen squirrels before, more than he could count, but you never knew what a squirrel was going to do and therefore every new one was worth watching.

There was a short, happy bark from Red as he dashed in pursuit. The squirrel hesitated a moment, until the big dog was almost upon him, and sprang easily to the bole of a tree. Red leaped, and reared with his front paws against its trunk.

"Come back here!" Danny shouted. "Red, you come back here!"

Ross turned to watch. "Why'n't you let him go after that little old squirrel?"

"Can't have him doin' it," Danny said stubbornly. "I don't want him chasin' those kinds of varmints. Red, you come back here!"

The squirrel scampered up the tree and disappeared in its topmost branches. With a final, wistful look toward them, Red came trotting in to grin sheepishly at Danny. Danny shook a finger at him.

"Red, doggone you! If you go off chasin' varmints thataway I'll . . . I dunno what I will do to you! How'm I goin' to make him stop, Pappy?"

"Give him a lickin'," Ross suggested.

"I can't. Red's not the kind of dog you can ever lick."

"Well, all I know is that if I had a hound chased things I didn't want him to chase, he'd get a hidin' that'd teach him not to. What's the matter with lettin' him chase them little varmints anyhow?"

"I don't want him to chase those kinds of varmints," Danny said desperately.

"You're teachin' him. Teach him your way."

Ross set off through the beech woods toward the creek, and Danny followed looking miserably at his father's back. The only kind of hunting Ross understood was that kind where you went out to kill something for practical use. But Ross had never been to a New York dog show, or talked dog with a man like Mr. Haggin. He was a good dog man, but with all his knowledge he just didn't understand that using a dog like Red for varmints would be like using one of Mr. Haggin's finely bred saddle horses to do a mule's work. Nor did he seem to know that it was impossible to take a stick or club and bludgeon every dog to the will of its master. Red was no ordinary dog. He was sensitive, high-strung, and a whipping would only make him hate or fear the person who gave it to him.

Danny shook his head. Red, being what he was, just naturally had to hunt partridges, and Ross would never understand that either. A partridge dog would be worse than useless if he left the hunt to chase whatever else crossed his path.

There was a rustling ahead, in a little patch of ferns, and Red sprang joyously forward to dive into them.

Ross broke into a little trot, and when Danny came up beside him he was looking at the brown entrance of a burrow in the center of the ferns. Red was digging with his front paws in the mouth of the burrow, and a little geyser of dirt spouted out on either side.

Ross said scornfully, "Your New York dog's tryin' to dig hisself out a woodchuck now, Danny. Talk to him, and tell him real gentle-like what a naughty boy he is!"

CHAPTER 5

RED'S EDUCATION

DANNY SHIFTED HIS FEET UNCOMFORTABLY, AND LOOKED from the growing pile of dirt behind Red to Ross. The big setter, shoulder-deep in the hole, came to a turn and swerved to dig in this new direction. Danny reached down to twine his fingers in Red's collar, and drew him out of the hole.

"Come out of there," he said as roughly as he could.

The big dog stood panting as he gazed eagerly back down the hole. He made a little lunge as though to get back in, and Danny took a firmer grasp on his collar. Red bent his head, snuffling at the hot scent of the woodchuck in the hole. He whined eagerly. Ross's frozen face melted.

"Don't look so miserable about it," he said. "All the dog needs is some more teachin'. Any tenderfoot dog worth its salt is goin' to chase any kind of varmint. But, what a varmint dog this'n'll make!"

Danny gulped wretchedly. "What should I ought to do about it, Pappy?"

"I'd give him a hidin'," Ross suggested seriously. "Now if'n he had a coon up a tree, I'd say let him go to it for all he's worth. But a varmint dog just can't stay at dens, and dig into every one he runs over. It takes too much time, and he's got to have a mind to stop it."

"But you can't give Red a lickin'!" Danny said desperately. "He's too smart and sensitive. Given I licked him he—he'd have no trust in me any more."

"Do tell!" Ross scoffed. "The dog was never born as didn't need to have sense licked into him at least once! But, as I said before, it's your dog. Bring him along and we'll get on with our fishin'."

Danny tugged on Red's collar, and the big setter strained backward toward the woodchuck hole. Danny dragged him from it, with Red protesting every step of the way, and when they had gone a hundred feet farther set him free. Red mounted an ant hill, and waved his plumed tail gently as he stared back toward the enticing den. Then he bounded to a moss-covered stump and smelled eagerly at it. Danny watched worriedly. A partridge dog had always to work within range of the hunter with him. And, of course, he must learn that partridges were the only game he could hunt. A dog that chased off after everything that crossed its path would be worse than useless.

But how to break him of this penchant for chasing varmints? Ross scoffed at the notion that a whipping would hurt him, but Danny knew better. Red had depths of feeling and sensitivity that he had seen in no other dog, and he was proud. He wouldn't bear the lash any more than would a proud man. Danny looked worriedly at Ross's back. Sometimes it seemed that taking care of a highly bred dog brought more perplexing problems than anything else.

A small buck with ragged shreds of velvet clinging to his nearly matured antlers stepped from behind a beech tree and stood looking at them. Ross halted. The wind shifted, carried to the buck the scent of human beings, and with a rasping snort and a mighty leap he hoisted his white tail over his back and bounded away. Ross lifted the fishing rod he carried and with the imaginary gun followed the buck's course. He turned to grin.

"I could of had him," he said. "I could of had him three-four times while he tore through the trees that-away."

"Reckon you could, Pappy," Danny agreed. He had

seen Ross bring down a buck running through slashings and a hundred yards away.

But he was studying Red, and heaved a great sigh of relief when the big setter betrayed no more than a passing interest in the buck. Deer scent, he knew, was the most pungent and exciting of any scent. Probably the hardest part of training any dog was to teach it not to run deer, and a dog that would run them was almost incurable. Danny had known of deer-running hounds to follow eagerly a scent two days old. But most hounds took naturally to running deer, and most setters would do so only if their interest in deer was deliberately encouraged.

Two hundred yards farther on they flushed a doe and her adolescent fawn, and Red merely looked at them. He fell in beside Danny, and Danny reached gratefully down to stroke his ear.

They came to a sunlit meadow with a tangle of blackberry briers at one end and lush wild hay carpeting the remainder. Smokey Creek brushed the far side of the meadow and broadened into a long pool deep at the upper end and shallow at the lower. The shiners Ross wanted swarmed in the pool, and there were a few big bass there. Trout occasionally came into the pool, but preferred the more secluded and shadier portions of the creek.

Red left Danny's side and darted swiftly forward. He paused to look back, then advanced another ten feet. Ross stopped perplexedly, studying the dog as he lifted one forefoot and held his tail stiffly behind him. Danny exulted, and some of the anxiety that had sat so heavily upon him since he had discovered Red's bent for chasing varmints departed. He knew these signs. Red was on partridges now, and if he was somewhat clumsy about it he still was not doing badly for a dog that had had no training. Danny laid the rod and can of bait he carried on the ground, and stooped to pick up a stone. He walked quietly forward, grasped Red's collar, and cast the stone into the small patch of blackberries at which he was pointing.

A partridge thundered up and soared across the meadow into the beech woods. Red whined, and twisted under Danny's restraining hand as he strove to follow. He reared with his front feet pawing the air. Danny held him.

"Easy," he murmured. "Don't get excited."

The big setter dropped back to earth and stood watching the place where the partridge had disappeared. As soon as Danny let him go, he raced out to cast around in circles and look for another bird. Danny watched him, leaping high in the tall grass so he could both see and scent, and turned to Ross with shining eyes.

"He had a partridge that time!" he ejaculated.

"I see he did." Ross looked disapprovingly at the ranging dog. "That's bad, Danny. A varmint dog shouldn't hunt nothin' but varmints. He sure oughtn't to go chasin' off after birds."

Danny said nothing.

Red came bounding back, and splashed shoulder-deep into the pool to lap thirstily at its crystal-clear water. He lay down to cool himself. A school of suckers moved sluggishly away from him, and a half dozen shiners darted erratically toward the bank, where they fell to nosing about the flat rocks that dotted the pool's bottom. Ross strung up his rod, baited the hook, and cast. Almost as soon as the line settled into the water a gentle tugging told of a bite. Ross struck, and his four-ounce rod curved slightly as he played a shiner in to the bank and slipped it into the live-bag that he had tied to a willow root beside the pool.

Red splashed out of the pool, stretched in the sun at Danny's feet, and went to sleep. Danny strung his own rod, cast, and almost immediately caught a fat chub. He put it in the live-bag, re-baited his hook, and caught another. There was no sport in catching chubs and shiners, but fish was the basis of almost every scent that he and Ross used on their far-flung trap-lines when winter came, and they took a major portion of their livelihood from trapping. For two hours they fished, until the live-bag was swarming with shiners.

Then, instead of the gentle tug that told of a shiner nibbling, Danny's line started straight across the pool. He let it go, feeling through the line and the wand-like rod that a big fish was on this time. The line stopped moving, and Danny waited tensely with two feet of slack looping from the reel.

"You better draw your line in," he warned Ross. "I got a bass out there fiddlin' with my bait, and he feels like a big 'un. Given I ketch him, we won't eat side meat for supper."

Again the line began to move, and Danny struck hard. Out in the black pool, where the taut line dipped into the water, there was a swirling little ripple. Far out, a gleaming, bronze-black bass broke water and splashed back in as he strove to shake the hook. He bore toward the bottom, and Danny paid out more line as he let him go. The rod, one that Ross himself had made, bent almost double. Danny elevated the tip, to let the fighting fish tire itself against the spring, and stripped in ten feet of line as the bass surged toward the bank. Red rose, and stood watching interestedly.

"Hang on!" Ross yelled. "He's a nice 'un!"

"I'm a-tryin' to," Danny panted.

The bass turned back into the pool, and Danny paid out the line that he had retrieved. Again the fish broke water, rising high above the surface and falling back into it. He began to run in little circles that grew shorter as he became more tired, and Danny played him toward the bank. Slowly he fought the bass into the shallows, and Ross waded out to stand knee-deep in the water. He ran his fingers down Danny's taut line, fastened them in the bass's gills, and lifted him triumphantly free of the pool.

"Four pounds!" he gloated. "Danny, I disremember any such bass taken from Smokey Creek before."

"He sure is purty," Danny agreed. "And he'll go plenty good for supper, huh?"

"You bet," Ross agreed. "What say we catch a half dozen more shiners and go home. It's nigh on to evenin' time."

They fished ten minutes, added six more to the bag of shiners, and dismounted their rods. The sun was sinking in the west, and a golden aureole glowed on the summits of the tallest mountains. Far back in the forests a fox yelled, and the wan, sad cry of a mourning dove came from the nearby beeches. But aside from that the forest was strangely hushed. Red ranged ahead of them as they walked homeward, sniffing at likely cracks and crevices wherever he found them, and when they passed the woodchuck hole he sniffed long and deeply at it. But few of the wilderness creatures were moving.

They came to the fence, and Danny lifted it to let Red crawl under. Ross climbed over, and Danny was about to do so when a rabbit burst from a bunch of thistle and went bounding across the pasture.

With a wild yell, Red was after it. The rabbit lengthened out, his white tail twinkling as he called on every bit of speed he possessed. Red flew, tail close to the ground and head up as he strove to overtake this enticing quarry. Chained to their kennels, the four hounds bayed loud encouragement. Even Asa, the mule, overcame his customary indifference to everything sufficiently to raise his head and watch.

Danny yelled, "Red, come back here! Come back!"

The big setter paid no heed, but bounded on after the fleeing rabbit. A half jump ahead of the dog, it flashed beneath a rock pile and disappeared. With his hind-quarters in the air and his front ones close to the ground, Red pawed futilely at the rocks. Danny ran up, grasped his collar, and jerked him roughly aside.

"You, Red! I dunno what I will do with you, anyhow!"

Ross walked up. "Goll ding it, I said I wouldn't meddle in the way you teach your dog. But he sure needs a hidin'. You let him sniff into dens and holes thataway, and he ain't never goin' to be no good for anything."

"Pappy, I won't whip that dog!"

Ross shrugged.

Red looked happily up, tongue lolling, tail wagging, and a bright, devilish gleam in his eye. Danny's heart melted. Red was smart, with all the heart and courage that anyone could ask for or expect to find in a dog. There must be some method, other than whipping, to wean him away from this sort of chasing and make him hunt partridges only. Danny gritted his teeth. It was up to him to find that method. He pulled Red into the house.

Ross took their catch of shiners into the shed, and began to prepare the trap-line scents that only he could make properly. Red went out to lie down on the porch. Danny skinned the bass, split it, and removed the heavy spinal bone. He laid the two halves in a pan of cold water and added a little salt. Red pushed the door open with his nose and came back in. Danny looked fondly at him.

"Rabbit-chaser," he murmured. "Darn old rabbit-chaser. When you goin' to get some sense into you?"

Red thumped the floor with his tail while Danny took the two halves of bass and laid them in a hot skillet. He sliced potatoes in another skillet, and put them on the stove to fry while he set the table. His hands covered with fish scales, Ross entered and washed. He took his home-made violin from its case, drew the bow across it a couple of times, and sat on a chair to coax from it the haunting strains of "Johnny O'Dare." Danny sang softly with him,

> *"Johnny O'Dare the moon is glowin',*
> *The silver clouds in the sky are showin',*
> *And I sit alone but alone am knowin',*
> *You'll come home to me Johnny O'Dare."*

He grinned. The day was gone, and with it all the doubts and perplexities it had brought. He, Ross, and Red, were alone with plenty to eat and a song in their hearts. It was enough. Danny put the cooked food on the table, and Ross returned the violin to its case. Both sat down to eat.

"What we goin' to do tomorrow, Pappy?" Danny asked.

"Mr. Haggin asked me to fetch him twenty-four quarts of blackberries," Ross said. "I better get at that come mornin'; he'll pay fifteen cents a quart. After that I won't be able to take any side jobs on account there's trap-lines that ain't staked out and I feel a ache for a varmint hunt. How would you like to chop down and trim a few trees for wood?"

"Sure. Fine."

Ross took a great forkful of the bass. "This is mighty tasty fish, Danny. By the way, do you consider that we should ought to let that Red dog run along when I take the hounds on a varmint hunt? Ol' Mike could teach him some tricks, and he's smart enough to pick up where Mike leaves off."

Danny choked on the food in his mouth. "I, I just don't favor the notion of Red's runnin' with hounds."

Ross looked at him, a little resentfully. "Well, it's your dog."

Danny went out to sit on the porch, while Red sat beside him and poked his nose into Danny's cupped hand. This was mighty serious. Ross had his heart set on making Red a varmint dog, and Red just couldn't be a varmint dog. It was in him to hunt birds, nothing else. Danny's right arm stole out to encircle the big setter's neck.

"You got to be a bird dog," he said. "You chase them little varmints because it's fun, but at heart you're a bird hunter. I sure wish Pappy'd understand. How we goin' to make him?"

Ross was already in bed when Danny re-entered the cottage and sought his own cot. And, though Danny was up with the sun, Ross had risen, prepared his own breakfast, taken his picking pails, and departed for the blackberry thickets. Danny milked the cow, fed Asa and Red, ate a great heap of pancakes, and took a razor-keen double-bitted axe from its rack in the closet. He went outside, strung Asa's leather and chain harness on the boney old mule, and hooked a long chain into the single-tree that dragged behind. Asa followed indifferently when Danny started toward a stand of yellow birch that had grown up in the beeches. Mr. Haggin, who owned most of the beech woods as well as the great Wintapi estate, didn't want any other trees cut as long as there was scrap wood like yellow birch around.

Red ranged before them, sniffing at likely thickets and bits of brush along the way. He came to a stiff point beside a clump of laurel, and held it while Danny flushed two partridges. Red made an eager little jump forward, and stopped. Danny forgot to breathe. The dog was smart, plenty smart, and getting the idea that it was not right to chase the partridges he pointed. Danny frowned. If only he would get the same idea about var-mints! But how to teach him without resorting to violent methods?

"I think you're doin' it out of devilishness alone," Danny murmured, more to himself than to the dog. "Doggonit, Red, why can't you stop?"

A hundred feet farther on Red had an ecstatic time chasing a chipmunk that was rooting in the fallen leaves for beech-nuts, and a little beyond he tore through the woods after a fleeing rabbit. Danny swung his axe and lopped down the thick weeds that had grown up beside the trail. Shouting at Red, as he had proven yesterday, did no good. Maybe, after all, he would have to use the choke collar and drag rope. He came to the stand of yellow birch, hitched Asa to one, and set to work fell-ing the slender little trees.

Most of the day he worked, chopping the birches down, trimming the branches from them, and piling them in a great heap. In the middle of the afternoon he untied Asa, led him to the felled trees, hooked the chain around a dozen of them, and tightened it. He led the mule back down the trail, left the trees in the chip-littered wood yard behind the shanty, and went back for another load. Dusk had fallen when he went down the trail with the last of the trees, and blue smoke was rising lazily from the cabin's chimney. He led Asa to the wood yard, and was piling the trees on those already there, when Ross came from the cabin to stand silently watching.

"You got a right smart lot of wood," he finally observed. "You better give Asa a feed of grain and rub him down, too. I'll have some vittles for you when you come in."

Danny cared for the mule, hung the harness in the barn, and with Red padding beside him entered the house. Ross bent over the stove, and when Danny came in he turned to smile wanly.

"I bet you got a yen for grub," he said.

"I could eat," Danny admitted. "But I'm not so tired. Tell me about yourself. Did you see Mr. Haggin?"

"Yup." With studied deliberation Ross turned away from him and faced the stove. "I took him his berries. By the way, Danny, he wants you should bring that Red dog and come down in the mornin'. There's some sort of quality woman stayin' there, and I guess he wants she should see him."

"Why, sure. It's Mr. Haggin's dog. He's got the right to see him if he wants."

"Danny . . ."

"What?"

"I . . . Set down and eat your supper," Ross finished

lamely. "You won't have nothin' else to do tomorrow. I'll take care of the wood you and Asa brought in."

"Two of us with a cross-cut'll get it sawed quicker," Danny said. "What's the matter with you, Pappy?"

"Nothin'. Set and eat."

Danny ate, and after eating strolled through the evening woods with Red while Ross washed the dishes. He was a little worried about his father. That Ross should even offer to wash the dishes was astounding in itself. Still, there didn't seem to be any physical difficulty; evidently Ross had something on his mind. When darkness fell, Danny went in to bed.

He was up very early, and scrubbed his face to the point of immaculateness in the tin basin. He put on a clean shirt and a fresh pair of trousers, and after breakfast, with Red frisking beside him, started down the Smokey Creek trail. A red fox leaped across the trail ahead of them, and Red dashed wildly to lunge at it. After ten minutes Red came back, panting heavily. Danny frowned and walked on. They broke out of the woods into the rolling acres of Mr. Haggin's estate, and started across them.

Red fell back to pace sedately at Danny's side, and Danny reached down to reassure himself by touching the dog's head. Of course Mr. Haggin was a mighty fine man, but just the same it was hard not to feel at least a little awed when approaching such magnificence as was to be encountered on his Wintapi estate. Danny saw two riders galloping on a pair of Mr. Haggin's blooded horses along a bridle trail, and looked carefully at them.

One was Mr. Haggin himself, and the other looked like a woman. Danny stopped in front of the barn. The two riders galloped in, and Red backed uncertainly against his knees. A groom came forward to take their horses, and Mr. Haggin and his companion swung from their saddles to come toward Danny. Mr. Haggin's booming voice bridged the distance between them.

"Good morning, Danny."

"Mornin', sir. I brought Red down."

Danny was studying the woman. She was tall, slender, and moved with the easy grace of a sable. She was dressed in riding breeches, polished boots, and a silken shirt. Her black hair had blown back on her head, and her cheeks were flushed. Certainly it was the quality woman of whom Ross had spoken. Yet Danny twitched uncomfortably. There was something very hard and very cold about her, as though she had always had her own way and always intended to have it.

"Miss Grennan, meet Danny Pickett," Mr. Haggin said.

"Hello, Danny," the quality woman smiled.

"Howdy, ma'am," Danny mumbled.

"Miss Grennan's the manager of my Philadelphia branch," Mr. Haggin explained. "There's the dog I was telling you about, Katherine, Champion Sylvester's Boy."

"Oh, Dick, what a gorgeous creature!"

The quality woman knelt beside Red, and put her hand on his ruff. Red backed a little nearer to Danny, to get away from the smell of the perfume she wore.

Danny looked at her with miserable eyes, knowing now why Ross had been so perturbed last night. The quality woman rose to her feet.

"Dick, give him to me."

"Whoa there! Wait a minute. What would you do with a dog like that?"

"Dick, let me have him."

Mr. Haggin coughed, and looked away. He squirmed, and coughed again. "Now, Katherine, your sense of acquisitiveness . . ."

"Oh, you silly! Let me have him for six months, and show him off in Philly."

"I can't let you have that dog."

"Why not?"

"Danny."

Katherine Grennan smiled again. "What do you say, Danny?"

"Well, I sure wouldn't like to see Red leave here."

The quality woman was very cold now, and very hard. "I know you wouldn't, Danny. But it isn't your dog, is it? It belongs to Mr. Haggin, doesn't it?"

Danny said manfully, "Yes, ma'am."

"There!" she said triumphantly. "Now let me have him, Dick."

Mr. Haggin looked at Danny. "Do you think she should take him?"

"It's your dog," Danny said.

"There, old iron man!" the quality woman said. "You can't have another thing to say. Anyhow, he'll be back in six months."

Mr. Haggin shrugged helplessly. "All right, Danny. Do you want to leave him now or bring him down in the morning?"

"Well," Danny hedged, "I could just as leave bring him in the mornin', and save you the bother of feedin' him tonight."

"Do that, Danny," the quality woman smiled. "I'll be leaving at eight o'clock."

With Red beside him, Danny turned miserably away. He swung from the trail to the foot of Misty Mountain, and started up its slope. When Red dashed after a squirrel, Danny only looked dully at him. The big dog might as well have his fun. Tomorrow morning he was going to Philadelphia, and that was almost as big as New York. There'd be no forest there, nothing except pavement and little patches of green grass that were called parks. With the back of his hand Danny wiped the tears from his eyes. The quality woman didn't really want a dog, or know what a fine dog was. She wanted Red because he looked nice, and would complement her own faultlessly groomed self. Every morning, probably, she would take him walking on a leash and the rest of the time he'd spend chained to some little kennel where there was just enough grass for him to scratch in.

It wasn't right to take a dog like Red away from the life he was meant for.

The bushes moved, and Red dashed happily in to chase whatever small creature was moving them. A little farther on he pointed two grouse, and Danny didn't even try to keep him from running after them when they flushed. All day he walked, up Misty Mountain, down its other side, and into the nameless gulleys and ravines that lay beyond. It was his last day with Red. True, the quality woman had said that she would bring him back in six months, but Danny didn't believe it. Once she got him, she'd find some excuse for keeping him. Darkness had fallen when Danny swung back to the clearing in the beech woods and stamped wearily into the cabin. Ross was there, sitting at the table and staring at the flickering kerosene lamp. He turned blankly around.

"The quality woman down to Mr. Haggin's," Danny explained dully. "Mr. Haggin give Red to her. She's takin' him come eight o'clock in the mornin'. I got to fetch him down then."

Ross nodded. "I figured she'd try to get her hooks in him given she saw him. I pegged her for that kind. What you goin' to do about it, Danny?"

"Take him down," Danny said hopelessly. "It's Mr. Haggin's rightful dog."

He sat miserably on a chair, pecked at the food that Ross put before him, and pillowed his chin in his hands. Ross filled and smoked a pipe, something he did only in times of great stress, and there was a long silence.

"You know what, Danny?" he said finally. "If I had the money cost of that dog, I'd buy him and give him to you."

"We haven't got seven thousand dollars," Danny said bitterly. "We haven't even got seventy dollars."

"That's right," Ross said tiredly.

Danny rose and sought his cot, praying for the sleep

that would not come. Sleep brought forgetfulness, and if he could forget for only a few minutes . . . But the long night hours dragged dismally and endlessly on. Just before dawn he fell into a restless and dream-troubled slumber from which Ross awakened him.

"Danny, I don't want to bother you. But if you have to be down to Mr. Haggin's at eight o'clock, it's nearly quarter past seven."

"Sure, sure. Thanks for wakin' me, Pappy."

Danny got out of bed and Red padded eagerly in to greet him with lolling tongue and wagging tail. Danny tore his eyes away from the big setter, and put on the clean clothes he had worn yesterday. There must be no fumbling or faltering now—unless the quality woman wanted to walk into the country back of Stoney Lonesome to claim her dog! Danny stooped to pat Red's forehead, and with an effort walked past him to linger in front of the door.

"I—I'll have some vittles when I get back, Pappy," he said. "Likely it won't take me long."

"Sure."

Ross turned around to stare out of the window. Danny opened the door, and Red raced happily out. He dashed at a rabbit that was nibbling clover at the edge of the pasture, and ran it under the stone pile. After scratching at the unyielding stones a few seconds he ran down the trail to catch up with Danny. Danny walked stolidly forward, turning his head away from the dog. A powerful magnet seemed to be pulling him toward Stoney Lonesome, where he could take Red and where Mr.

Haggin and the quality woman couldn't find him if he didn't want to be found. But that wouldn't be right. Red was Mr. Haggin's dog, and Mr. Haggin had a perfect right to do with him what he would.

Some tall grass beside the trail moved, and Red raced joyously down to investigate. He jumped into the grass, remained a moment, and came stumbling out. For a bit he stood in the trail, and rubbed his face in its gravelled bottom.

Danny said sternly, "Heel."

He marched steadily on, not looking around. Red had had his last run after a varmint. When he got to Philadelphia there might be a cat or two for him to chase. But certainly there would be nothing more. Danny took a deep breath, and plunged out of the forest onto Mr. Haggin's estate. He saw Mr. Haggin, standing with one foot on the running-board of a smart roadster, and the quality woman in it with her hands on the wheel. She looked curiously around, as Mr. Haggin said,

"Good morning, Danny."

"Mornin', sir."

The quality woman took a silk handkerchief from her purse and held it delicately against her nose. Red backed against Danny's knees, and Danny steeled his aching heart. The big setter did not want to go. But he must go. Danny stooped, put one arm around Red's chest and the other about his rear legs. He lifted him bodily, and deposited him on the polished leather seat beside the quality woman.

"Here's your dog, ma'am," he murmured.

Suddenly and violently the quality woman recoiled. She grimaced, grabbed the silk handkerchief with both hands, and plastered it against her nose.

"Get that thing out of here!" she gasped.

Red hopped over the side of the car, and squeezed very close to Danny's legs. The woman turned furious eyes on Mr. Haggin, whose face had turned purple and whose mouth was emitting subdued gurgles.

"Dick, if this is your idea of a joke . . . !"

"Now, Katherine, I swear that I had nothing whatever to do with it."

The quality woman put her car in gear, stepped on the gas, and gravel spurted from beneath the wheels as she roared toward the road. Mr. Haggin gasped, and burst into gales of uncontrolled laughter. Danny watched wonderingly.

"Oh Lord!" Mr. Haggin said at last. "That's the best I ever saw! Katherine thought she knew everything, and found out that she still has something to learn. Take your dog and go back up into the beech woods, Danny. He's safe now."

But Danny had already gone, was racing up the Smokey Creek trail on winged feet, with Red gambolling happily beside him. A small rabbit hopped across the trail, and Red made a wide circle around it. Danny burst into the cabin.

"Pappy!" he yelled. "Pappy, I got Red back and I'm goin' to keep him. He don't chase varmints no more, either; he wouldn't run at a little old rabbit in the trail. That quality woman, she's gone and she don't want him, just because on the way down he jumped on a skunk! Can you imagine anybody not wantin' a dog like him just because he smells?"

Ross's eyes were shining, but he shook his head gravely. "City women are funny thataway," he observed. "I'm so glad for you, Danny. But you better take your dog down to the crick and wash him off. He do smell a bit, but in a couple of weeks you won't hardly notice it a'tall."

CHAPTER 6

THE LEAVES RUSTLE

THE SUMMER DAYS FADED LIKE GOLDEN SHADOWS ONE into the other, and the first frost came to leave its delicate traceries on the earth and a riot of color behind it. Danny went into the deep woods with Ross, packing loads of traps and caching them in hollow stumps and caverns where all traces of man scent would be eliminated. He climbed mountains and travelled streams, blazing with his axe every place where a set trap might take a fur-bearing animal and getting ready for the long winter to come. But, when he was not doing that, he was abroad with Red.

The big setter had learned his most important lesson well, and no longer chased whatever ran before him or leaped on bushes when they moved. Slowly, bit by bit, he became woods-wise, and as soon as he had learned that partridges were the game desired, he worked conscientiously on them. He had that all-important requisite of a shooting dog—the willingness to enter whole-heartedly into the spirit of the hunt, and when his roughest faults were smoothed over, he learned fast.

Danny taught him to quarter before him, always staying within sight, to respond to the wave of a hand when Danny wanted him to hunt cover to the left or right, and always to obey whatever other commands were given. The dog heeled perfectly, lay down on command, and remained there until instructed to get up. With difficulty Danny taught him to return to the house, leaving Danny in the woods, when told to do that, and started him retrieving with a soft ball. And, when he was finished, he knew that he was going to have a partridge dog.

Red was not perfect; it would take a season in the field and birds shot over him to make him perfect. Danny thought longingly of his shotgun, and the few birds he would have to shoot to give the big dog his final lessons. But the season was not open yet. He and

Ross had never broken game laws, and he was not going to start now. Red's final training would just have to wait until it was legal.

With Red frisking before him, Danny tramped out of the beech woods on a frost-tinged evening in early autumn, and into the cabin. Ross was sitting at the table, his chin in his hands, staring out the open door at the haze-shrouded peak of Stoney Lonesome. Ross's four hounds had come out of their kennels, and each sat at the end of its chain staring at something that only they could see. Danny grinned. It was this way every year. When summer started to fade Ross worked hard and long to prepare for the trapping season. But little by little he became impatient, and by the time the first frost struck impatience would be a raging fever within him. Then he must take his hounds and go into the mountains for the season's first varmint hunt.

"Danny," said Ross, "do you think the trap-lines are in good shape?"

"Sure they are. We got a right handy lot of trappin' laid out for us." Danny grinned to himself.

His father resumed his staring out the door, while Danny busied himself preparing the evening meal. Ross was a proud man and a hard worker, and little was ever permitted to interfere with essential work. Because varmint hunting was his pleasure, he hesitated to go while there was other work to be done.

"Supper's ready," Danny announced.

Ross moved moodily over and sat down, staring at the food before him. Danny watched him covertly, and a little anxiously. Ross had been working very hard, and his eyes showed it. But he was still trying to convince himself that there was work to be done on the trap-lines, and he could not possibly take a varmint hunt. Danny stopped eating, and said carelessly,

"Pappy, if the hounds are goin' to be in shape for the winter, they got to have some chasin'."

"Yeh, I know," Ross said absently.

"Then," Danny continued, "why don't you take 'em out for a varmint hunt, come mornin'?"

"Well, there's a little work to be done on the Lonesome Pond line . . ."

"You can't be caught in the winter with soft hounds," Danny warned.

"By Joe!" Ross slapped the table with his fist. "That's right, Danny. Guess I'd better take 'em out!"

"Sure. It's just as important as trappin'. You catch a lot of varmints with those hounds."

"That's right," Ross repeated. "Can I take the Red dog with me, Danny?"

Danny fidgeted. "That Red, I gotta work him some more."

"Mebbe so. I'll take him the next time."

Danny washed the dishes and read the latest issues of the outdoor magazines while Ross prepared happily for his hunt. Danny went to bed early, and when he awoke Ross had taken the four hounds and gone into the mountains. There was a roughly pencilled note on the table:

"Danny, don't worry if we ain't back tonight. If we jump a long runner, we may stay two days."

Danny went out on the porch to look at the weather. The maple tree in the pasture, under which Asa and the black and white cow rested when the sun shone hot, had streaks of red running through its leaves. The leaves on the beeches hung listless and yellow. A cold wind blew down from Stoney Lonesome, and Danny whistled happily. Autumn was surely the finest time of all. Partridge season opened in just a little more than three weeks, and he could go shooting with Red. Afterward he and Ross would lay in their winter's supply of venison, and when the deep snows came they'd don snowshoes and hit the long trails into the back country. Spring and summer in the Wintapi just couldn't compare to fall and winter.

Danny prepared breakfast, fed the big setter, and did the few other chores that needed doing. Then he took a pack basket from its hooks on the shed wall, and dumped thirty number-one steel traps into it. Ross was worrying about the Lonesome Pond trap-line, but he could stop worrying when he came home to find it all finished. That was the last line; all the others were ready.

Danny shouldered the basket, and the big setter frisked happily before him as he set off through the beech woods. The cold wind sighed down from Stoney Lonesome, and far off Danny thought he heard the mournful baying of a hound. He stopped to listen, but the sound was not repeated. Red walked toward a small hillock that was carpeted with wintergreen, and looked invitingly over his shoulder. But Danny snapped his fingers.

"Come back here, dog. There's work to be done."

He strode up the valley, following the course set by Smokey Creek through the huge beeches. A buck deer, with the last shreds of summer velvet gone from its branching antlers, stood silently as a wraith in the trees before him. The buck snorted, stamped the ground with a forefoot, and bounded away. A couple of crows cawed raucously from the top of a beech, and flew on the devil's business that their kind are always about. Then Danny broke through the last of the beeches on to Lonesome Pond.

The beech woods ceased abruptly, and in an almost perfectly straight line flanked the edge of a weed-grown meadow. Here and there, ragged tamaracks reared their green heads through the great expanse of withered cattails and bulrushes that lined the suddenly widened valley.

The pond itself was a mere widening of Smokey Creek, a mile and a half long by a half mile wide. Lonesome and sluggish, it rested between the acres of reeds and was flanked by the straggling tamaracks. It was a desolate place, but the little, conical houses that muskrats had built were strewn thickly wherever there was shallow water, and freshly cut reeds floated almost everywhere. Every year Ross and Danny took a hundred muskrats from the pond, and caught eight or ten mink on the little mud paths around it. Danny knelt to examine the bank.

Muskrats had been digging there, coming out of the water to root for the succulent bulbs that grew so abundantly around the pond. Danny deposited his pack on the bank, and went to one of the discouraged tamarack trees. With his knife he cut half a dozen forked branches from it, and from a grove of willows beside the pond took twenty more. He returned to the water, took a trap from the basket, and thrust one of the sticks through the ring at the end of its chain. He drove it deep into the bank, pounding the fork down until nothing showed, and cast the trap into the water. Even muskrats were sometimes wary and hard to take. But they would become accustomed to the trap by the time the season opened, and pay no attention to it when it was set.

Danny worked slowly around the pond, leaving an unset but firmly staked trap at every likely place. He already knew the narrow paths under the banks where wandering mink ran, and he set the basket down forty feet from the first one. Red looked questioningly at him.

"Down!" commanded Danny.

The big setter crouched by the basket, and Danny took out a trap. He waded into the water, thirty feet from where he was to make the set, and made a long half-circle toward the spot. Careful to touch nothing that might retain human scent—mink were among the wariest of beasts—he staked the trap chain in the water. Then, with the blade of his axe, he lifted the trap onto the path and splashed water over it. He and Ross would be along later to set the traps, but when they did they would use deodorized gloves.

The sun was sinking when Danny straightened up from the last trap and swung the empty pack basket to his shoulders. He sighed, and stretched his cramped muscles. But the Lonesome Pond line was finished and ready. There remained only the setting of the traps. Danny grinned down at Red.

"I feel like supper. How 'bout you?"

Together they walked back to the cabin in the beech woods. But the kennels were still empty; Ross was not back. If he didn't come before dark it meant that he would not be back. But it was best to give him an hour or so more. A man who had been tramping through the mountains all day would be hungry, and appreciate a hot meal.

With Red beside him, Danny walked out on the porch and sat on the top step sniffing hungrily at the fresh breeze that eddied about the cabin. It was just right, and smelled just right, with a strong hint of more frost and the barest promise of snow to follow. A straggling V-line of geese flew over the cabin, and their quavering calls drifted back down to it. Red raised his head with Danny to watch, and fell to sniffing at the bird-laden beech woods that began where the pasture ended. Danny pulled his ear.

"Stop sniffin' for partridges," he admonished. "We can't shoot 'em now anyhow."

In spite of his advice, he rose, and with Red circling happily ahead of him walked down the steps. The big dog snapped to a stiff point before a little group of pines that had somehow managed to find a root among the beeches, and when Danny advanced two partridges thundered out. Red danced on eager feet, watching them soar and disappear in the beech woods. Danny swung toward the barn, and passed it to enter the forest. The sun was almost gone now and the huge, gloomy trees, that had already shed a fair portion of their leaves, stood in the dank chill of an early autumn evening. Danny threaded his way through them to Smokey Creek.

Its dark waters curled around the beech roots, running alternately in quiet, leaf-laden pools and leaping riffles. Danny knelt to read in the mud bank beside the creek the story of the wayfarers that had been most recently along it. A she coon had led her family along the stream, and under the small stones in a little back-eddy they had caught crayfish. The restless trail of a wandering mink mingled with that of the coon family; he also had been fishing. A muskrat had been digging in the bank.

Danny wandered back to the house, cut chops from a side of pork in the spring house, peeled a kettle full of potatoes, and brewed fresh coffee. The day had been pleasantly warm, but the night was definitely cold, so he stuffed two blocks of tough oak wood into the stove. The lid glowed red, and the pleasant aroma that wood fire always creates filled the cabin. Danny put the potatoes over to boil, and laid the pork chops in a skillet. Probably Ross would not come. But he might, and if he did he would expect a hot meal ready. When the potatoes began to bubble, Danny moved them to a back lid and put the pork chops in their place. If Ross didn't come to eat his share, Danny could always make breakfast on whatever might be left.

He stood over the stove with a fork in his hand, and was just about to turn the sizzling pork chops when Red sprang to his feet. A little growl bubbled in his throat, and his hackles raised. Danny shoved the pork chops to the back of the stove and went to the door.

A moment later he saw Ross swing out of the forest into the clearing and start across it. Ross's rifle swung from his hand, and the pack was on his shoulders. Danny swallowed the lump that rose in his throat and went quietly back to the stove. His father's hunt had gone amiss. Of the four hounds that had started out with him that morning, only three were coming home. The missing one, Danny knew, lay somewhere in the mountains and would never hunt again.

Twenty minutes later Ross entered the house. Danny had known that he would be that long; having had hounds in the mountains all day, Ross would take time to feed and care for them before attending to his own wants. Red rose, and padded politely across the floor to greet this other occupant of their home. Danny turned from the stove, and the cooked supper, to smile at his father. He knew better than to question Ross about his hounds.

"Hi, Pappy. I didn't know for sure whether you'd get home or not."

"Yep. I got here."

Ross's face was haggard, as were his eyes. Wearily he hung his rifle beside Danny's, sloshed water from one of the two tin pails into a tin basin, and washed his face and hands. He dropped on a chair and sat staring dully across the table. Danny tended busily to the already cooked pork chops, and glanced furtively at Red. Ross Pickett set a lot of store by his hounds, and it always cut him deeply to lose one. With the long fork Danny put the pork chops on a platter, and emptied the potatoes into a dish. He set them on the table along with butter, milk, and bread, and tried to make his voice gay.

"Supper's ready, Pappy. How'd it go today?"

Ross Pickett shook his head. "Bad, Danny, bad. I lost a hound."

"No!"

"Yes," Ross corrected. "The likeliest of the three pups it was, too."

"How'd you lose him?"

"Killed by a varmint, a cat varmint. We jumped him in that sag just under Stoney Lonesome, and I heerd the hounds bay him a mile back in the brush. Time I got there, they'd gone. The pup lay by a rock, ripped to ribbons. We followed the varmint all day, but I never got a shot."

Danny said, "I'm right sad about it, Pappy."

Ross pecked at the food before him, still staring aimlessly across the table. Danny busied himself with his own food, avoiding his father's face. Whoever hunted dangerous game with hounds was sure to have one killed once in a while. But Ross always grieved over such mishaps, and blamed himself for them. He picked up a pork chop, gnawed on it, and put it back on his plate.

"It's a big cat varmint, Danny," he said. "A big lynx or catamount."

He resumed his vacant staring over the table. Never given to futile outbursts, he would not now storm and rage. But Danny knew that his present moodiness was not wholly grief. The varmint that had killed the hound was still running free in the mountains. And even while he mourned the loss of one of his cherished dogs, Ross could still lay plans to avenge it. Danny knew that he was plotting the varmint's downfall now, and also that he was quite capable of pursuing it until he finally did overtake it, regardless of when that might be. No varmint of any description ever killed a Pickett hound and went scot-free.

Danny finished eating, and sat silently at the able until Ross, by pushing his plate aside, signified that he wanted no more. Danny flipped the half-eaten pork chops to Red, and the big setter carried them to the porch where he lay gnawing on them. Ross turned the kerosene lamp a little higher. He took his best hunting knife, one that he himself had made of tool-steel and that was always reserved for special occasions, and began to whet it on the fine side of an emery stone. The next time he went into the mountains he would carry that knife, and its next function would be to remove the pelt of the varmint that had killed his favorite pup. Danny shivered. There were grim depths in his father that only an occasion such as this could bring to the surface.

Quietly Danny gathered up the dishes, poured hot water from the tea kettle into a basin, and washed them. He glanced dubiously at his father, still sitting at the table whetting his knife to a razor edge. Ross raised his head, and stared fixedly at the flickering lamp before he spoke.

"Danny, I think that's a bad varmint."

Danny listened attentively as he always did when Ross spoke of varmints. He had hunted them all his life, and certainly no man knew more about them. Ross rested his chin on his hand.

"I do think so," he said, more to himself than to Danny. "It's no ordinary cat. It trapped that hound, and waited until it could trap it without hurt to itself. Then it got slick and clean away. It's a cunnin' thing, and a big one, and I think it aims to make itself boss of Stoney Lonesome. Danny, do you go up there, you carry a gun."

"I won't go without I'm ready for it," Danny promised.

"Don't," Ross admonished.

He fell to whetting the hunting knife again, and Danny stood uneasily watching him. Tomorrow morning, with his three remaining hounds, Ross would be again on the trail of the varmint. There was no use in even asking to accompany him because Ross would flatly refuse all aid. The varmint was a personal affair, and one that concerned him only.

"Guess I'll go for a walk," Danny said.

"Sure. Go ahead."

Danny walked down to the creek with Red, and took a swing through the beeches. When he came back to the cabin it was dark. Without striking a light Danny sought his own bed. In the black hours of the next morning, so early that the first hint of dawn had not even begun to show in the sky, he was awakened by Ross kindling a fire in the stove. Danny lay sleepily on his cot, and reached over to caress Red, while he watched his father prepare breakfast. Ross ate, and made a small pack in which he put bacon, salt, bread, and tea. He rolled the pack in his fringed hunting jacket, slung it across his shoulder, strapped the knife about his middle, and took his rifle from the rack. Quietly he stole out the door and closed it behind him.

Danny heard Old Mike, the leader of the hound pack, whine eagerly as Ross went to the kennels to release the hounds, and his father's gruff command to be quiet. Then there was silence, and Danny turned over to sleep until a more reasonable hour. There was nothing special to do today, aside from splitting a little wood, and therefore no reason to be up so early.

When he awoke again, sunlight was streaming through the windows and a bluejay in the maple tree was shrieking invective at the mule. Red padded over to Danny's bed and scratched with his front paw at the blanket that covered it. Danny looked at Ross's empty bed, and the space on the deer horn rack that was usually occupied by Ross's rifle, and sighed. Ross would be far back in the mountains by this time, looking for the trail of the varmint that had killed his hound. Danny swung out of bed, and opened the door to let Red make his usual morning tour of the clearing. He washed, put on his clothing, and was preparing breakfast when he heard Red bark.

The dog barked again, and a series of challenging barks rolled from his throat as he ran toward the Smokey Creek trail. Danny reached for his rifle, and went to the door. Red stood just at the edge of the clearing. There was motion within the trees, and Red trotted forward with his tail wagging. A moment later John Bailey, the game warden who patrolled the Wintapi, broke out of the trees and with Red beside him started toward the cabin. He paused at the bottom of the steps, and grinned up at Danny.

"Are you going feuding?"

Danny grinned back. "Pappy had a hound killed by a varmint yesterday, and he allows it's a bad 'un. When I heard Red, I just thought I'd be set for anything. That's how come I got a gun."

John Bailey nodded. "What kind of varmint?"

"A cat varmint. Pappy's back in the hills huntin' it now."

"Hope he gets it," the warden said thoughtfully. "We can't have any cats killing deer in the Wintapi. Danny, are you too busy to do a little job for me?"

"Reckon not. What do you want?"

"There was a big buck hit by a car on the highway yesterday afternoon. Almost certainly he has a broken leg and internal injuries. But he isn't hurt so badly that he can't run. I tracked him a ways, to Blue Sag up on Stoney Lonesome, and marked where I left off with a handkerchief. He laid down three times, and there was blood in each bed. Do you want to pick up the trail and finish him?"

Danny nodded. A wounded beast, left alone, would run until it thought itself safe from pursuit. Then it would lie down, usually to suffer days of agony that would only end in death. It was far better to put the buck out of its pain as swiftly and mercifully as possible.

"Sure," Danny agreed. "Red and I'll go after him."

John Bailey reached down to tickle Red's ears. "Aren't you afraid the dog will learn to hunt deer?"

"No, sir," Danny said stoutly. "That dog hunts just what I want him to."

"Okay. When you get the buck, bring him here to your house and I'll come get him. Of course the meat will have to go to a hospital or the county home, but I'll pay you for your time."

"Sure thing."

John Bailey disappeared back down the trail, and Danny took his own rifle from its rack. He gave Asa a measure of oats, milked the cow and put the milk in the spring house, packed a lunch, and with Red careening happily before him set off through the beech woods toward Stoney Lonesome. A gray squirrel scampered around the side of a tree, and Red looked interestedly at it but let it go. He glanced back at Danny, and grinned foolishly. Danny grinned back. Red had learned his lesson well.

Danny toiled up Stoney Lonesome's steep slope, and halted before a huge, grey-trunked beech to get his bearings. Red stopped beside him, sitting on the ground with his plumed tail outstretched. A pileated woodpecker hammered on a tree, and a chipmunk with his cheek pouches stuffed full of beech nuts dived backward off a stump. A little gust of wind blew across the forest floor, and ruffled the fallen leaves. Danny cut a little to the left, and came to the edge of the shallow gulley that was called Blue Sag. He stood on the rim, his eyes roving up and down. Red walked into the gulley, sniffed interestedly along it, and raised his head suddenly to stare toward one of the big blue rocks from which the sag took its name. Danny's gaze followed his, and he saw a corner of John Bailey's white handkerchief beside the rock. Danny snapped his fingers and called Red to him.

"Heel," he ordered. "If there's tracks, I don't want 'em messed up."

With the dog walking behind him, he made a slow way to the rock and knelt to study the ground. A low whistle escaped him. John Bailey hadn't exaggerated when he called this a big buck. The imprint of its cloven hoofs were huge and plain beside the rock. But there was a little line where it had dragged one hind foot, and it had fallen twice in climbing out of Blue Sag. Danny put his hand in the scuffed leaves, and brought it away wet with blood.

"He's hurt, right enough," he murmured to himself. "It looks like he's hurt mortal bad. But he might go a smart piece yet."

He followed the trail to the top of Blue Sag, and stood pondering. Badly injured, the buck would not be likely to climb any hills or seek any other hard going. He would choose the easiest way, and that was straight around the rim of the mountain. If he deviated from that course he would go downhill. Danny followed the trail, walking swiftly where scuffed leaves made it plainly visible and painfully studying it out where the buck crossed hard or rocky ground. Red walked beside him, and when he would have gone uphill to hunt some partridges that he smelled there, Danny called him back.

By late afternoon they were far around the side of Stoney Lonesome, in a region of big and little boulders. The buck was walking more slowly now, and lying down more frequently. But he was only a little way ahead, floundering and working mightily to keep away from the pursuer that he knew was on his trail. Danny kept his rifle poised, ready for the first shot that might offer.

Then he walked around the edge of a boulder and placed his foot within six inches of the prostrate buck. For one brief second he had a glimpse of a huge, tortured gray body surmounted by a superb rack of horns. In split-second decision he raised his rifle and shot. At exactly the same second the buck, able to run no more and prepared to fight, hurled himself up and over. Danny scrambled wildly, and felt his flailing hand brush the side of the boulder. His head thudded against the rock and blackness enfolded him.

When he awoke it was night. His head throbbed painfully, and a great weight seemed to be crushing his right foot. For a few seconds he lay quietly. There was motion beside him and Red's anxious whine sounded in the darkness. Danny flung out a hand, found the dog, and felt Red's wet tongue licking his arm. Slowly he raised himself to a sitting position, and as soon as he did that his head cleared.

But when he tried to move his right foot, he could not. It was bent around the boulder, and held there in an unbreakable grip. Danny fumbled in his pocket for the box of matches that he always carried, and struck one against the boulder. In its wavering glare he saw the buck's head, upper body, and one of its huge antlers. The other antler was pressed tightly against the rock. Danny gulped. The antlers ended in a wide fork, and when the deer had thrown itself over on its back the fork on the right antler had closed over his leg, then wedged itself deep into the earth and against the rock to form an almost perfect trap.

Danny moved a little down the hill to ease the strain. Sweat rolled from his forehead, and sharp pain travelled the length of his body as he strove with all his strength to pull himself loose. But the dead buck did not even move; the antler that pinned his foot was firmly wedged. Danny sat up, and leaned forward. By extending his fingers he could reach around the edge of the rock and touch the dead buck's throat and muzzle. But there was nothing on which he could get a firm hold. He lay back down.

"No time to lose your head, Danny," he murmured to himself. "You can't do a thing by flyin' off the handle."

A sharp wind blew around the side of Stoney Lonesome, and fluttering leaves rustled. Red snarled fiercely and rushed, barking, into the night. Danny whistled him back.

"Don't get excited," he murmured. "Little old leaves a-blowin', that's all. Take it easy Red."

Suddenly Danny was afraid. That wind would carry all along the side of Stoney Lonesome, and blow leaves before it. It would cover whatever trail he had made so thoroughly that nothing could follow it. Nobody, not even Ross, could guess exactly which way this buck had come or where he was. A search party would certainly be organized, and in time would find him. But how much time would that take? Danny felt as far as he could in every direction, but his groping fingers could not touch the rifle. Probably he had flung it when he fell.

He snapped his fingers. Almost immediately Red stood over him, half-seen and quivering in the darkness. The dog lowered his cold nose to touch Danny's cheeks, and whined. Danny lifted a hand to stroke his shoulder.

"Listen," he said, slowly and emphatically. "Listen careful, Red. Go home!"

Red whined and backed away. Danny waited eagerly, his fingers crossed and an unsaid prayer in his heart. If Red went home alone, Ross would know that something was amiss. He would also bring Red with him when he came to look for Danny, and almost certainly the big setter would lead him back here. But Red only sat on his haunches and bent his head down.

"Go home!" Danny ordered angrily. "Go home!"

Red whined again, and stood up to face into the darkness. The wind increased, and another gust of leaves blew around the side of the hill. A snarl rippled from the big setter's throat, and again he raced, barking, into the darkness. Danny felt cold despair creep through him, and then anger. For the first time Red had shown a flaw. Afraid of leaves blowing through the darkness! Danny choked back the sobs that rose in his throat. Red emerged from the night to lie beside him, and Danny brought his right hand up to cuff the dog on the head.

"Go home!" he yelled. "Go home!"

Red backed a few feet away and sat down uncertainly. Danny writhed on the ground, but the antler that imprisoned him could not be moved. He was as helpless as if he had been tied.

"No time to lose your head," he repeated. "If that fool dog won't go home, think of somethin' else."

But there was nothing else except the darkness, the great pain in his foot, and the long, endless minutes. He bent his head toward the dog, and snapped his fingers. Red came cringing in to lie beside him, and Danny stroked his back.

"I'm sorry, Red," he muttered, "sorry I hit you. But, oh dog, if you'd just go home!"

The long night hours dragged painfully by, and twice more the leaves rustled. Each time Red ran, barking, into the darkness. At long last gray morning spread itself across the sky. With it, so suddenly and unexpectedly that Danny jumped, came the clamor of hounds. They were very close, baying within a few hundred feet of where Danny lay. Ten minutes after they arrived there was the sharp snap of a rifle. Danny sat painfully up and shouted.

"Hall-oo-oo!"

And he heard Ross Pickett's answering, "Hall-oo!"

Danny sat very still, listening to the rustling leaves that told him his father was on the way. He saw Ross, followed by the three hounds, appear among the trees and toil up the hill. Ross knelt to examine Danny's foot, and the swift concern on his face changed to a grin.

"It's what you get for shootin' deer out of season. But you ain't hurt bad. How long you been here?"

"All night."

"I'll get you out."

Ross caught the dead buck's antlers and heaved upward. Danny felt his foot come free, and rolled gratefully over. He sat up, and leaned forward to watch Ross massage his cramped foot. Red stretched full length in the leaves and watched approvingly. Danny glanced reproachfully at him.

"I'm sure glad you came, Pappy," he said. "I thought you might be home, and tried to send that fool dog there. But he wouldn't go. Mebbe he ain't as much dog as I thought he was. Every time the leaves rustled, he ran towards 'em barkin' like all get out. A dog, scared in the dark! 'Tain't right."

For a moment Ross looked steadily at him. "I got the varmint," he said at last. "It's a big lynx."

"Yeah? I heard you shoot. How'd you get him, Pappy?"

"I kept the hounds on leashes, and slow-tracked him

all day and all night," Ross said soberly. "When the trail freshened, I let the hounds go and they bayed him. Danny, that trail freshened within five hundred yards of where you're sittin' now, and there wasn't no low wind to rustle the leaves last night. That varmint was studyin' you, and the smell of the dog, and the smell of that dead buck, all night, and tryin' to figger if he was safe. It was him you heard, rustlin' the leaves when he came towards you. If it hadn't been for your dog . . . How you goin' to make it up to him, Danny?"

But just at that moment Red came forward, buried his nose in Danny's cupped hand, and closed his eyes blissfully while Danny scratched his ears.

There was nothing to make up.

CHAPTER 7

PARTRIDGE DOG

FOR A WEEK, AFTER ROSS HAD HELPED HIM BACK FROM the side of Stoney Lonesome, Danny hobbled about the cabin with his right ankle swathed in bandages that were regularly soaked in an epsom salt solution. The Picketts could seldom afford a doctor, and even though they now had the fifty dollars a month that Mr. Haggin was paying Danny to take care of Red, it never occurred to either of them to pay another man to do what they could do themselves.

Every day Ross went into the hills, sometimes taking his hounds with him but more often walking the lonely trap-lines that he and Danny had already staked out, his eyes alert for possible improvement. Ross seldom rested, and never wasted time. As far back as Danny could remember he had been doing something, trapping, varmint hunting, digging ginseng, picking berries, collecting wild honey, or some of the dozen other jobs to which woodsmen turn their hands. Ross had always secretly dreamed of having fine things, luxurious things, and from the start was doomed never to get them. But he never seemed to recognize the fact that he was doomed, and always tried to bring as much as he could into the shanty in the beech woods.

Red stayed with Danny, loafing around the cabin, going out to make restless tours of the clearing, or venturing a little way into the beech woods. But he never got very far away or stayed very long. Wild to be off and hunt partridges, the big setter still waited loyally until Danny was able to go with him.

Danny had skinned the big lynx that had stalked him throughout the long night on Stoney Lonesome when his foot was pinned beneath the dead buck's antler. The huge pelt was on a stretching board. There was a twenty-dollar bounty on it, but the big cat had been killed so early in the year that its pelt was all but worthless. It was going to be Danny's after the bounty was collected, and he planned to make it into a wall decoration.

At twilight on the seventh night, Ross came stalking into the clearing with the three hounds trailing behind him. They crawled to their kennels, were fed there, and then Ross came stumbling into the house. He sat down, and smiled wearily at Danny.

"How'd it go?" Danny asked.

Ross shrugged. "All right. I kept the hounds off the trap-lines on account I don't want the traps smelled up with dog smell, and we went into some of them valleys 'way back of Stoney Lonesome. The hounds hit a trail, and went barkin' off on it. For the life of me I couldn't make out what they was chasin'. I let 'em go, and kept as close behind 'em as I was able. They treed and I come on 'em. Do you know what they had up, Danny?"

"What?"

"A big, spittin' fisher cat," Ross grinned. "He was only 'bout ten feet up in a pine, cussin' the dogs and tellin' 'em what he was goin' to do to 'em if he got a mind to come down. When I got there he run 'way up in the tree and hid. I could of had him though, and would of 'cept his pelt wasn't prime. You should of seen him, Danny. He's black as the ace of spades, and silky as all get out. He'll be worth a sight of money when the winter puts a pelt on him. I'm goin' back there, come mornin', and spy out some of his runs so he'll be easy to catch."

"Gee," Danny sighed. "I'd like to of been with you. I haven't seen a fisher cat for two-three years."

"They ain't so plenty," Ross observed. "But I'd as soon kill what I run across on account they kill so many other things. When this one gets primed up, we'll have us a fisher hunt."

They ate supper, cleaned and repaired a faulty ejector on Ross's rifle, and went to bed. Danny slept late, but Ross was up with the dawn and off to locate some of the fisher's runways. Red, who couldn't understand why Danny should suddenly decide to loaf about the house instead of going as usual into the more interesting woods, came in to paw at his bed and wake him up. Danny grinned, and before he dressed stooped to take the bandages from his ankle. Gingerly he rested it on the floor, and finally put his whole weight on it. It pained a little, but he could stand and walk with only a slight limp. Danny mixed pancake batter, and was about to cook some pancakes when Red growled warningly. There was the sound of someone walking.

"Hey, Danny," a voice said.

Danny looked around in surprise. His visitor wasn't the casual trapper he had expected, but Mr. Haggin. The owner of the great Wintapi estate wore a pair of blue jeans, a faded gray shirt, and his sockless feet were encased in leather moccasins.

Danny blurted, "I didn't know it was you, Mr. Haggin."

"Yup," Mr. Haggin grinned. "I'm going away to-morrow, heading south, and thought I'd drop in on you."

"You're mighty welcome."

Mr. Haggin looked worn and tired, as he glanced around the neat cabin. Danny watched, puzzled. Mr. Haggin had money enough to buy himself anything he wanted, and he'd hardly look enviously at a trapper's cabin in the beech woods. No, it was not exactly that. Rather it was as though Mr. Haggin had wearied of something, and come here to find peace. Money, Danny decided, could not buy everything. Then Mr. Haggin looked at Red, and the weariness faded from his eyes. He spoke enthusiastically.

"If he'd been in that shape when we took him to New York he'd have won best in show, Danny."

Danny relaxed. Mr. Haggin wasn't a millionaire any more. He was like Ross, or any other man who could know and love a good dog. But Mr. Haggin knew more about some kinds of dogs than Ross had ever dreamed. Very clearly there rose before Danny the vision that was never far from him. He remembered the dog show, down to the least detail, and the great triumph he had felt when Red won best of breed. But still there seemed to be something lacking from that show.

"Red looks right good," he agreed. "I was thinkin' . . ."

He hesitated, and Mr. Haggin asked, "What were you thinking?"

"Why, I was thinkin' that there'll be more dog shows to come," Danny said lamely.

"You and I think alike, Danny. Do you remember the little bitch that went up with Red for best of breed?"

"Oh!"

"Yes," Mr. Haggin sighed. "And there still isn't

enough money to buy her from Dan MacGruder. But I'm keeping my eyes open. As soon as I can get hold of a good enough bitch I'll send her up here. There'll be dog shows next year, and the year after, and twenty years from now."

"Yes, sir," Danny said soberly. He glanced at the stove and asked, "Would you like some breakfast?"

"Sure thing," Mr. Haggin said. "What have you got?"

"Flapjacks."

"Wahoo! It's been a long while since I've sunk my teeth into a good mess of flapjacks. My cook calls 'em —never mind. It's an insult. Have you got maple syrup too?"

"Pappy tapped the trees and boiled the sap himself."

"Lead me to it!"

Danny cooked a great platter of flapjacks, and put them on the table. He opened a can of maple syrup, poured a pitcher full, and set it before Mr. Haggin. Mr. Haggin took a plateful of the flapjacks, spread butter on them, drowned them in amber maple syrup, and ate. He took another plateful, and ate more slowly while Danny told him all about Red, the big setter's partridge hunting, and all the hopes he had for him. When he was finished, Mr. Haggin leaned back in the chair.

"Now I've got something to remember," he said. "But I've also got to go. I'll see you in the spring, Danny."

"Yes, sir. I'll take good care of Red."

"I knew that three months ago," Mr. Haggin said. "Good luck, Danny."

They shook hands, and Mr. Haggin strode back down

the Smokey Creek trail. Danny sat on the top step of the porch, watching him go. Red came to sit beside him, and Danny pulled his ears. He was vaguely troubled because the memory of the dog show would not leave him, and he still was unable to identify positively the thing that should have been there and was not. It seemed to be another dog. Of course, no matter what happened there was never going to be another dog like Red. But . . .

Danny stamped back into the house and washed the dishes. He went to the wood lot, took a buck-saw from its hanger, and began to saw into stove-length blocks the trees that Asa had dragged out of the woods. Red sat near, watching. Danny worked doggedly on, trying by hard labor to drive from his mind the troublesome thought that refused to be driven. It was four o'clock in the afternoon when Red, who had been nosing around the wood pile, barked sharply. Danny looked up and saw Ross run out of the beech woods into the clearing.

Ross's hat was off, and he carried his jacket in his left hand. His face was red from exertion, his eyes glowed with excitement. Red ran to meet him. Danny dropped the buck-saw and stood erect. Ross panted to the wood shed, and leaned against the door to catch his breath.

"Danny . . ." he said.

Danny grasped his arm, and looked concernedly into his father's face.

"What's wrong, Pappy?" he asked.

"I—I went back in the ridges," Ross gasped. "I went back to look for the fisher cat, and I found his runs. But

I was standin' on the side of a little stinky gully, and the wind was to me. I looked over and I saw that big hellin' bear, Ol' Majesty. He ain't been in these woods sinst you and that Red dog run him out. But he's here now! He was feedin' off a dead deer, and when he finished feedin' he crawled in a hemlock grove. Danny, that bear's got his belly full and he ain't goin' to move before mornin'. That Red dog bayed him once, and he can do it again. I'll take him up there come dawn and put an end to that raidin' bear!"

Danny turned away. Old Majesty, unforgiving and terrible foe of every man in the Wintapi, was back again. Soon he would be raiding again, and this was a chance to kill him. He should be killed. Danny looked at Red, and swallowed hard. Red had bayed Old Majesty once, and might do it again. Only . . . Danny straightened. Ross had his heart set on making Red a varmint dog, and Danny had no intention of letting him hunt varmints. That issue had to be faced some time, and it might as well be now.

"I reckon not, Pappy."

"What!"

"I—I guess Red ain't goin' to be no varmint dog."

"Huh! What use would you put such a dog to?"

"Well, he could hunt partridges."

"Them little brown birds? You're funnin'! You wouldn't waste such a dog on partridges."

Danny said desperately, "Look, there's some things a man can do and some he can't. Makin' Red hunt varmints would be like makin' one of Mr. Haggin's

blooded horses do Asa's work. It's right in Red's blood
to be a partridge dog."

"Oh. Did Mr. Haggin tell you to make him hunt
partridges?"

"Mr. Haggin didn't say anythin'," Danny said miserably. "I just know Red's a partridge dog."

"How do you know it?"

Danny tried and failed to put into words some of
the things he had learned on his brief visit to New York
and in his association with Mr. Haggin. Always before
he had accepted Ross's notion that a dog was a dog,
something to be bent to the will of its master. But that
wasn't so. For thousands of years there had been special
dogs for special functions, dachshunds for entering
badger holes and subduing their occupants, greyhounds
for coursing swift game, malemutes for sledge work,
and only when you knew something of their blood lines
could you really appreciate the fascinating story of dogdom. It was in Red's blood to hunt birds, and partridges
were the only game birds in the Wintapi. Making him
hunt anything else would verge on the criminal. But
how to explain all this to Ross?

"I just know it," Danny said miserably. "Red hunted
the bear only because he thought it was goin' to hurt
me."

"Well, if that's the way you feel . . ."

Ross went stiffly into the cabin and prepared supper.
After eating, he helped wash the dishes and took his
accustomed place beside the stove. He ignored Red
when the big setter tried to thrust his nose into his

cupped hand and, sensing the rebuff, Red went back
to Danny. Danny sat moodily alone. Ross was deeply
hurt. He would not have been had Danny been able to
furnish a single good reason why Red should be a partridge dog. But Danny himself knew of no reason save
that Red had been born to hunt partridges. And that
sounded silly.

They went silently to bed. The next morning, when
Danny got up, Ross had already gone. He had taken
one of the hounds with him. But he hadn't asked Danny
to go along.

Danny's heart was heavy within him while he ate a
lonely breakfast. But after eating, he opened the door
and a flood of the sparkling October sunshine came
spilling in. Red rushed outside, and went over to sniff
noses with Old Mike. He came galloping back to Danny
and reared to put both front paws on his chest. Danny
pulled his silky ears, and stroked his smooth muzzle. If
only Ross was there to see Red as Danny saw him! Then
the autumn and the sunshine worked their magic. It
was enough to be afield with Red. Ross would understand in time.

Crisp, frost-curled leaves crackled underfoot when
they entered the beech woods. Red went racing among
the trees. But when Danny whistled he stopped, turned
around, and came trotting back. For a space he walked
beside Danny. Then he leaped a few feet ahead and
stopped in his tracks.

He stood with his body rigid and his tail stiff behind
him. With a quick little rush he went a dozen feet and

stopped again. Then in a slow, steady walk, he advanced twenty feet and stopped on a knoll. He raised one forefoot, stiffened his body and tail.

"Easy. Easy there, Red," Danny murmured, very softly.

The dog trembled, but held his point. Danny leaned over, and as quietly as possible brushed the leaves from a half-buried limb. He hurled it into the brush at which Red was pointing, and a lone partridge thundered out. Red took three nervous steps forward, but halted at Danny's, "Back here, Red."

Danny's knees were suddenly weak and he sat down. Red came over with wagging tail and lolling tongue, and Danny passed both arms about his neck. Starry-eyed, he sat still, in his mind living and re-living the scene he had just witnessed. It was a thrill to hear hounds strike a trail, to listen to them baying their quarry, and their final frenzy when they cornered it. But this! The hounds were good workmen, but the setter was an artist. And not even Ross had suspected how keen his nose really was. Danny rose.

"Come on, Red."

They found three more partridges. On the second, Red broke a little. But on the third he was more steady and the fourth he held perfectly. Danny gasped anew each time. Red was scenting the birds at such distances and holding them so well that even seeing it was hard to believe. But four were enough without any shooting. Making any hunt tiresome was a certain way to spoil a dog. Danny took Red for a walk high up on Staver

Plateau, where only sweet fern grew and there were few grouse. A sullen resolve that was forming in his mind reached fruition there. If Ross didn't want him on the trap-lines he certainly wasn't going to beg to be taken along! He didn't have to trap. The fifty dollars a month Mr. Haggin was paying him was more than enough to meet his share of their common expenses. He swung down the plateau toward home.

The early autumn twilight was just dimming the day when he arrived. A light in the window told that Ross was there before him. Danny opened the door, and Red slid unobtrusively in to lie on the floor. Ross, who was standing over the stove, turned and spoke briefly.

"Hi-ya."

"Hi-ya," Danny replied, and busied himself setting the table. From time to time he stole a furtive glance at Red, and once looked with mute appeal at his father's back. But his eyes squinted slightly and the same stubborn mouth that was Ross's tightened in grim lines. Once more he looked at Ross's back, and found the determination not to speak until his father did, melting away. Danny tried to make his voice casual.

"Where'd you go today, Pappy?"

"Out."

Danny flushed, and his face set in stubborn lines again. Maybe Ross thought he couldn't make a partridge dog out of Red. He'd show him! He'd prove such a dog much more valuable than a hound, and every bit as practical. But proving to Ross that any partridge dog was worth the food he ate wasn't going to be any easier job than moving Staver Plateau with a toy tin shovel.

After supper Danny sat by Red for a while, stroking his ears and tickling his chin. But Ross ignored the dog completely. And, as though he understood, Red had nothing to do with him.

Partridge season and the first snow came together. Ross, as usual, was up long before daylight and away on his trap-lines. When Danny went out with his shotgun and Red, he looked longingly at the tracks in the snow. Always before, he and his father had gone trapping together. Resolutely he shouldered his gun and walked in an opposite direction, toward the pine and hemlock thickets where the partridges would certainly seek shelter from the snow.

They approached a thick growth of hemlock, and Red ranged ahead. He came to a stiff point, and Danny edged up.

A partridge burst out of the hemlocks, showed itself for a split second between the branches, and Danny shot. A ruffled heap of brown feathers, the bird came down in the snow. Red hesitated, looking around at Danny as though asking for instructions. Danny waved a hand forward.

"Go on," he said. "Get him."

Red padded forward, and stood uncertainly over the fallen partridge. He looked up, and back at the bird.

"Give it to me," Danny said gently.

The setter lowered his head to sniff the partridge, and grasped it gently in his mouth. Danny took it in his hand. He threw it down in the snow and Red picked it up again. They went on, and Red pointed three more grouse, which Danny shot. The last one, though Red went about it in an awkward fashion, he picked up and brought back. His tail wagged furiously and his eyes glistened at the lavish praise that the feat called forth from Danny. But four birds were the limit.

Danny arrived home first that night, and had supper ready when Ross came in. Ross had no furs, as he had set his traps only that day, but he opened his hunting jacket and took out four partridges. He laid them on the table, and turned silently away to remove his coat and wash his hands.

Danny's cheeks burned. Ross had had no dog. And every one of the four partridges had been shot through the head with the little .22 pistol that he sometimes carried on his trap-line visits.

The partridge season wore slowly on, and by the last day Danny knew that his hunch had been the correct one. Red was not only a partridge dog, but he was a great partridge dog; one in a million. He found the birds and pointed them so carefully that only the wildest ones flushed before the gunner could get his shot in. It had taken him only nine trips afield to learn perfectly the art of retrieving. Regardless of how thick might be the brush or brambles in which the bird fell, Red would find it. And, though he had hunted every day, Danny had not yet lost a wounded bird. Red paid no attention to the rabbits that scooted before him, or to the chattering squirrels that frisked in the trees. And, when he hunted, no scent save that of partridges drew the slightest interest. Now, on this last day of the season, he and Danny were going out for one last hunt.

Ross, as usual, had already gone, and a few flakes of snow hovered in the air. Little wind stirred and the naked trees were silent. But the blue-black horizon and the clouded sky foretold a heavier storm to come. Danny went back into the shanty and buttoned a woollen jacket over the hunting shirt he already wore. He dropped half a dozen twelve-gauge shells into his pocket.

"Goin' to be weather, sure enough," he murmured. "Winter's nigh here, Red."

The hard little snow flakes rustled against the frozen leaves, and it seemed to Danny that they were falling faster even before he came to the edge of his father's field. But he forgot them then because Red came to a point. Steady as a rock, he stopped just a little way within the woods. Danny flushed the bird. It soared up and out, dodging between tree trunks and twisting about. But for one split second it showed through the crotch of a big beech and Danny shot. The bird dropped to the ground and Red brought it in.

They went on, deeper into the beech woods where they had found so many partridges. But Red worked for an hour before he pointed another, and that one flushed so wild that Danny had no shot at it. It was noon before he killed another, and at the same time he awoke to the necessity of getting back to the cabin before he had trouble finding it. The snow was falling so fast that the trees were only wavering shadows. And there was a rising wind, which meant that the heavy snow would be accompanied by a gale. Danny snapped his fingers. "Here, Red."

The dog came in reluctantly. His ears were flattened, and his tail hung dejectedly. He knew as well as Danny that they should have killed four birds. And he considered it his fault because he had found only three. Hopefully he started once more toward the hemlocks. But the boy turned toward the cabin.

The wind whipped his clothing about him, and drove snow into his eyes. He bent his head and turned his collar up. There was a foot of snow on the ground, and all open places were drifted waist-deep. Red stayed behind, following the trail Danny broke, and floundering through the drifts.

It was nearly dusk when they reached the cabin. Danny opened the door, stamped the snow from his feet, and sank into a chair. Red crouched full length on the floor, looking at Danny from the corners of his eyes. The boy grinned, and went over to pull his ears.

"Wasn't your fault, you old fool," he said affectionately. "You found what there was to find."

Red leaped happily up and went over to sit beside the door. But Danny took his jacket and hat off, and draped them over a chair. He started a fire in the stove, and shook his head.

"Nope. Not again. We got all we had comin', anyhow. There's a passel of canned partridges in the cellar as'll come in right handy if vittles get scarce."

Red returned to his place on the floor and lay disconsolate. Danny cut thick slices from a ham, and peeled a great pot full of potatoes. Ross would be hungry after bucking the storm, would want good things to eat and plenty of them. But Danny worked with deliberate slowness, trying in the accustomed routine of household chores to still the small worried voice that was crying within him. Ross should have been home before this.

He went to a window and peered into the inky blackness, fighting back a rising panic. This was no time to lose his head. He waited another ten minutes.

Then he made up a pack: a thermos of coffee, enough food for three days, a knife and axe, plenty of matches, and two woollen blankets. He put on his warmest coat, pulled a felt cap down over his ears, and took his snowshoes from their peg on the wall.

With a happy little whine and a furiously wagging tail Red sprang up to join him. Danny looked at him. The dog could not be of any use. He would hunt only partridges, would pay no attention to Ross's scent, even though they passed within ten feet of him. Danny shook his head.

"Reckon not, Red. This here's one hunt I got to run alone."

Red flattened his ears, and begged mutely. Danny looked away and back again. Red wouldn't help any. But he would be company, and certainly could do no harm.

"All right. C'mon."

Danny went outside, and Red waited impatiently in the snow while he took a toboggan from its elevated platform. When Danny started off through the night, the dog ran a little ahead. Danny watched him work carefully toward a brier patch, and grinned wryly. Red was still ashamed of his inability to locate more than three partridges, and was trying to make up for it.

The snow was drifting down in great feathery flakes that dropped softly to earth. The wind had abated and it was not as cold as it had been. But if Ross was helpless, he could freeze. Danny put the thought from his mind and plodded grimly on. Lately, he had scarcely spoken to his father, but he still knew where to look for him. Last night Ross had brought in two muskrats and a mink, pelts that could be trapped only along waterways. Therefore he must have run the traps in Lonesome Pond. Today he would cover the fox line on Stoney Lonesome ridge.

But, even though he would search until he found his father, Danny was aware of the near hopelessness of his mission. If Ross was lying unconscious, after having been caught in a slide or struck by a falling limb, the snow would cover him, and he might not be found until it melted. Danny clenched his fists and tried to drown the thought. Ross was too good a woodsman to have such an accident. But, Danny admitted, nobody was too good at anything to guard against unforeseen accidents. It was just as well to face possibilities as to close his eyes to them. He must be ready for anything.

Red came trotting happily back, and was away again. As Danny dragged the toboggan up the long, steep trail his father took to Stoney Lonesome, he looked down at his feet. They seemed barely to move. Yet he saw by a dead stub beside the trail, that served them as a land-mark, that in an hour he had come almost three miles. That was fast travel in deep snow when a man had to drag a toboggan.

It was too fast. A quarter of a mile farther on Danny stopped to rest. He panted heavily, and sweat streamed down his face and back. He took the felt hat off and opened his jacket. Red returned to stand anxiously beside him.

"If only I'd taught you to hunt men instead of partridges," Danny half sobbed. "If only I had!"

He turned to go on. Ross had to be somewhere, and he was as likely to be near the trail as anywhere else. But if he wasn't, his son would go to all the traps, and from them he would branch out to scour every inch of Stoney Lonesome. Ross couldn't die. Why, there would be hardly anything worth while if it wasn't for his father. That foolish quarrel over Red! Danny should have let him hunt varmints or anything else Ross wanted. If only he could talk to his father just once and tell him how sorry he was!

Danny stumbled, and sprawled in the snow. He rose, angry and shouting. He had fallen over Red, who had come to a point in the trail.

"Go on!" Danny snapped.

Red took three uncertain steps forward and stopped again. Danny rushed angrily toward him. He reached down to grasp Red's collar, but the toes of his snowshoes crossed and he stumbled forward again. His bare hands plunged deeply into the snow. They hit something soft and yielding, something that gave before them. It was a man's trousered leg. Danny dug frantically, and lifted Ross Pickett from his snowy bed. His hand went under Ross's shirt.

His father was warm and his heart still beat.

*   *   *

The next day, back at the cabin, Danny served his father two roasted partridges and a great heap of mashed potatoes. He propped Ross up on pillows, and grinned when his father began to wolf the food.

"For a man as should of been dead, you're sure hungry," he observed. "How come you can eat so much?"

Ross grinned back. "Can't kill an old he-coon like me." He tore off a great strip of breast meat and held it up in his fingers. "Come here, Red. Come here and have some vittles."

Red padded daintily across the floor, and his wagging tail thanked Ross for the offering. Danny's eyes shone, because the two things that he loved best now loved each other. Ross looked at him.

"'Twas a mighty lot of foolishment to fight over the dog, wasn't it? But even if I hadn't got over my mad, like the mule-head I am, and was waitin' for you to say somethin', I sure would know what a pointin' dog is now. When that old trail give way beneath me I thought I was a cooked goose for certain. How come the dog found me, Danny?"

Danny said soberly, "Red found you on account he's got a better nose than any hound dog."

It was the first lie he had ever told his father. But it was more evasion than lie. Red was a partridge dog through and through. And, when he had pointed there in the snow, he had pointed not Ross, but the two partridges Ross had shot and put in his pocket.

CHAPTER 8

READ THE SIGN

THE NEXT MORNING DANNY AND RED RAN THE TRAPS IN Lonesome Pond, and brought back two muskrats and a mink. Ross was sitting in front of the stove, bent over. He straightened up, revealing a red flush in his cheeks and dry, cracked lips. Ross tried to get up, and caught the back of the chair. He spoke with forced casualness.

"How did it go? Did you take some pelts, Danny?"

"Two 'rats and a mink. You're sick, Pappy!"

"Me!" Ross scoffed. "I ain't been sick in twenty years!"

"Well, you are now." Danny left his fur-laden coat on the porch. "Come over here, Pappy."

Ross said stubbornly, "I'm not goin' to bed."

"Now you just quit actin' like a two-year-old and use your head!" Danny scolded. "What good's it goin' to do if you get yourself pneumonia?"

"Aw, it's a foolishness."

"Sure!" Danny said sarcastically. "A man as has laid under a snowdrift for five or six hours shouldn't ought even to feel it. Get in bed, Pappy."

"Oh, all right! I'd rather than have you jawin' at me!"

Ross took off his clothes and crawled into bed. Danny felt his hot temple, then took from the cupboard a quart bottle of whiskey that had stood there unopened for five years. He broke the seal, poured a water glass half full, and filled the glass with hot water.

"Drink it," he commanded.

Ross drank, grimaced, and sputtered. "Whew! You're either goin' to kill or cure a man, ain't you?"

"Stay covered," Danny ordered. "If you're not better by the time two hours has gone, I'm goin' to call Doc Smedley."

"It'll cost you twenty-five dollars to get him 'way up here!" Ross protested.

"I don't care if it costs two hundred and fifty," Danny said. "We can't have you sick."

"It's a foolishness," Ross mumbled. He settled drowsily down in the blankets. "John Allen was here. He wants you should help him get his cows out of those grass meadows up on the plateau. I told him you'd help. He'll give you a quarter of beef for the helpin'."

"I—I can't help him," Danny protested.

"Why not?"

"I got to run the Stoney Lonesome line come mornin'. Deer season opens next day, and I got to get us a buck for winter meat. Next day I got to go back to Lonesome Pond."

"Stoney Lonesome'll wait," Ross said. "It's mostly a fox line, and there ain't goin' to be too many foxes runnin' for two-three days after that storm. You help Allen in the mornin', get your buck next day, and go up Stoney Lonesome the day after if you have to. Course, I think you won't have to on account I can go up myself by then."

Danny said severely, "You're goin' nowhere until you're well. But I'll help Allen anyhow."

Danny pelted the muskrats and the mink, skinning them carefully and stretching them on boards that were exactly suited to them. Furs were much more valuable if they were properly handled. He inspected his work critically, and went back into the cabin. Ross was asleep. Some of the angry red was gone from his cheeks and his forehead was cooler. The next morning he ate three soft-boiled eggs that Danny prepared for him and drank a bowl of warm milk. He got out of bed to sit in front of the stove, while Danny fumed.

"You fuss like an old settin' hen with sixteen chicks," Ross observed drily. "I'd rather be up than down."

"You should be in bed, Pappy."

"Ah, I'll just set here. The minute I get tired, I'll go back to bed."

"Well . . ."

"I knew you'd see it my way," Ross smirked. "You go on and help Allen; he said he'd meet you in the meadows."

"All right. The mule's fed and the cow's milked. I'll go. But if you're worse tonight, I'm goin' to call Doc Smedley anyhow."

"Shucks. No need to do that."

"Take care of yourself and I won't have to."

"I'll take care of myself."

"Well, you been warned."

Danny put on his hat and coat, and with Red beside him went outside. For a time he pondered the advisability of wearing snowshoes, but the snow in the valley was only eight inches deep. Only in open places where the wind had a long sweep had it drifted. Of course it would be deeper in the uplands and on the tops of the mountains, but not much, this early in the winter. Danny left his snowshoes on their hanger, walked down the valley, and climbed the face of Staver Plateau.

A cold wind blew up the slope, and carried a dusting of fine snow with it. The snow already there was almost knee-deep, but the ranging cattle had beaten paths through it. Danny broke out of the forest into the meadows, great open stretches carpeted with wild hay and grass, and leaned against a stump. In the distance a herd of ten cattle came out of the forest into the meadows, and turned to race back to the shelter of the trees. Danny grinned.

"There they are, Red. Some of John Allen's gentle bossies."

Every spring John Allen, a Wintapi farmer with only small acreage of his own, bought forty or fifty cattle, barren cows, calves, bulls, steers, and let them graze in these wild uplands. Every fall, shortly after snow flew, he rounded them up and sold them.

There was a hail from down the slope, and Danny looked that way. A man with a woolly shepherd dog beside him had come out of the trees into the meadow, and was toiling upward toward Danny. Red rose eagerly, and bounded through the snow to meet and sniff noses with Shep, John Allen's cow dog. Side by side the two dogs wagged up to Danny, and John Allen panted along behind them.

"Been waitin' long?" he asked.

"Not so long. What's new?"

"Not much. One of them jail people they got over at Downdale broke prison. Have you seen any cattle?"

"I just saw ten of your wind-splitters, John. They took one look at me and kited back for the brush."

"Shep'll get 'em back," the farmer said confidently. "What side do you want, Danny."

"I'd as soon take the other. Give me half an hour."

Danny followed one of the winding cow paths around the face of the hill, went through the little strips of forest

that separated the various meadows, and took a stand
where the unbroken forest began again. The cow path
petered out in a great area of pawed snow, where the
cattle had been digging for grass. Danny climbed a
hundred feet above it, and sat watching. Shep would
rout the cattle from their bedding and feeding places,
then they would run like the wild things they were. It
was Danny's job to keep them out of the forest and
headed downhill. There was a wingfence there that led
into a corral.

Presently he heard a dog bark, then a succession of
hurried barks. Ten minutes later a little grey bull with
a dozen cows and calves behind him came racing along
the path. Red pricked up his ears, and Danny ran down
to stand in the path. Seeing him, the bull braced his feet
and stood with lowered head. Suddenly Red's thunderous battle roar burst from his throat, and he hurled
himself forward. The grey bull stood his ground for a
second, then turned, and with his cows and calves following plunged down the hill.

Red ran a little way after them, nipping at their heels
and chivvying them on, then turned to come panting
back to Danny. Danny grinned, and tickled his ears.

"They wouldn't of hurt me, you old fool," he said affectionately. "But if you've took it in your mind to be a
cow dog, go right ahead. We'll get 'em down quicker."

He waited until he heard the questing Shep barking on a level with him, then ran swiftly down to the
next path. Six black and white heifers came racing along
it, but Red had already learned the game. He sprang

happily at them, his eyes alight with mischief, and chiv-
vied them down the hill into one of the strips of forest
that separated the meadows.

Bit by bit they worked down the hill, and as the cattle
were driven below, Danny swung slowly toward the
other side of the meadows. The scattered little bunches
of cattle gathered into a herd that galloped away whenever he approached. Shep came racing, driving five
yearlings before him. They joined the herd, and disappeared with it into a forested ravine that led down the
slope. Shep ran back to hustle a reluctant bull from its
cover, and Red joined in the heel-nipping as they drove
the bull into the ravine. Both dogs disappeared, but their
steady barking floated back to Danny. Red-faced and
panting, with little tobacco-juice icicles hanging from
his walrus mustaches, John Allen appeared on the other
side of the ravine.

"Any get past you, Danny?" he called.

"Nary a one."

The other man grinned. "I heard your dog barkin'.
Was he rousslin' them cattle along?"

"Yeah. He's gone down the ravine with Shep."

"Let 'em go," John Allen said. "It's where I want 'em.
They think they're awful smart, gettin' in that wooded
ravine. But it runs right into my wingfence, and comes
out in the corral. We got 'em goin' our way, Danny."

"I'll take your word for it."

Side by side they walked down the ravine, and found
the two dogs sitting together in the gate of the corral.
Fenced at last, the cattle were milling about. A few awk-

ward, spraddle-legged calves were standing still and facing outward. John Allen closed the gate, and Red came wagging back to Danny. He was surprised to find the sun sinking and the valley in shadow. There had been swift action nearly all day, and time had flown quickly. John Allen leaned on the gate with his hands folded.

"There they are," he said. "Tell Ross that I'm goin' to butcher the biggest and fattest steer, and I'll bring him a hind quarter. Will you come down to my place for supper, Danny?"

"Thanks," Danny said, "but I ought to be gettin' back. Pappy's sick."

"I know he is. Let me know if I can do anything."

"I will. So long."

"So long, Danny."

Danny followed one of the cow paths back up the slope, cut around the nose, and retraced the tracks he had made that morning. He ran the last five hundred feet up the valley, and stopped running, reassured, when he saw the cabin. Ross was all right, for blue smoke was curling from the chimney. Danny entered, and Ross grinned at him from the bed.

"Your supper's warmin' on the stove, Danny."

"How do you feel, Pappy?"

"Half dead," Ross said disgustedly. "Half dead from uselessness. Did you git all of Allen's cows hazed out of them meadows?"

"Every one, down to the last spindlin' calf."

"What in tunket has Red been doin'?"

"Chasin' cows. He got himself full of stick-tights. But I'll comb him after supper."

Danny felt his father's forehead, which was still hot but lacked the raging fever of yesterday. He ate his supper, washed the dishes, and spread a newspaper on the floor. Red sprang up to stand in the center of it when Danny took a comb and brush from a shelf, and shivered in delighted anticipation. Red didn't like baths, but loved to be brushed and combed. Danny worked carefully over him, removing every burr, bit of dirt, and all the loose hair. In the flickering light cast by the kerosene lamp, Red gleamed like burnished copper, and from the bed Ross smiled wan approval.

"The more I see that dog the better he looks, Danny," he said.

"Yep." Danny stood up, and Red moved off the paper. Danny stooped to roll it up and thrust it in the stove. He put the brush and comb back on the shelf, and Red padded over to rub his combed flanks against Danny's legs and look in mute appeal up at his face. Danny grinned, and stooped to scratch his ears.

"You old lap dog," he said. "Always want to be petted, don't you?" He left the dog and walked over to the bed. "Can I get you somethin', Pappy?"

"Nah. I'll be up and around in a couple of days, mebbe less."

"You will not!" Danny said. "And you won't be outside until your cold is plumb gone."

"Yes, sir," Ross said meekly. "Did Allen have anything new to say?"

Danny shrugged. "Nothin' special. There was a jail break at Downdale, and Allen said he'd send our beef up here."

Danny took his rifle from its rack and sat down to oil the action. He looked through the barrel, to make sure that nothing obstructed it, and swabbed it out with a ramrod. Carefully he counted out ten shells, and set them in a row on the table. Red padded happily over, and stood with his eyes level to the table, looking at the shells.

"You aimin' to down a buck, huh?" Ross asked wistfully.

"Yup."

Danny kept his eyes averted from the bed. Ross was aching to go deer hunting. But he couldn't, and Danny had to. The venison they got every year was an important food staple to the Picketts. No doubt Ross would be well enough to go out and hunt the last part of the season. But the deer would be wild and scattered by that time, and regardless of how good a hunter he was no man could be sure of a buck. Red came over again to rub his combed flank against Danny's shins, and Danny played his fingers over the big dog's back. Of course he would take Red with him, not to help hunt deer but for company.

"Don't you worry," he said. "You'll get your chance at a buck, wait and see. I bet you'll get a bigger one than I do."

"Sure," Ross gulped, and then grinned. "Don't even trouble your head about me. I'm no tenderfoot deer hunter, as has to git his game the first day or he don't git it."

"Go on now," Danny scoffed. "Quit your braggin'."

Ross said soberly, "You better git to bed, Danny. You mebbe got a long day ahead of you."

Danny was up long before dawn the next morning. He milked and fed the cow, fed Asa, cooked breakfast for himself, gave Ross what he wanted, and packed a lunch. Danny put on his red jacket, and pinned a strip of bright red cloth to his hat. For a moment he stood awkwardly, looking at the helpless Ross. Then he filled his rifle with five cartridges, dropped five more into his pocket, and with Red crowding close beside him went out on the porch.

The night was lifting slowly, reluctantly. An inch of new-fallen snow was piled against the barn and spring-house, and lay in smooth mounds on the branches of the beech trees. Old Mike, leader of his father's hound pack. came out of his kennel and stood in the snow lifting one paw after the other, only to crawl back into the warm kennel. Red ran down the steps, and sniffed at a pile of snow-covered weeds. A resting rabbit burst out of them and left a tiny tracery of tracks as he dashed away over the new-fallen snow. Red watched him go, and came back to Danny.

Danny waited, standing quietly on the porch while the darkness faded and the daylight gathered strength. There were great herds of deer in the Wintapi, but if you wanted to be sure of getting one you had to figure on a hard and careful hunt. On the other hand, deer often grazed down to and bedded at the very edge of his father's clearing. It was possible to jump one almost anywhere, and a man who went too early into the forest could easily miss some fine chances. Danny shuffled his feet to warm them, and spoke softly.

"Meat hunter," he accused himself. "You're just a darn old meat hunter."

But that was all right, too. City hunters who could afford to come three, four, or five hundred miles to hunt in the Wintapi, were well able to hunt for sport alone. But, though both Danny and Ross enjoyed hunting and hunted fairly, neither could afford to overlook the fact that the creatures they hunted also furnished them with a great share of their food. Meat hunting was nothing to be ashamed of, Danny decided.

He raised the rifle, and sighted on a thistle that rose brown and naked above the blanket of snow. The front sight blurred, just a little, and Danny took the gun down again. Cartridges cost ten cents apiece, and there was no sense in using three to do the work of one. Unless the sights could be clearly seen, you never could be sure of your aim, and it would stay dark longer in the forest than it would out here. Danny waited ten minutes and raised the gun again.

This time he saw the sights clearly, and could even discern the frost-shrivelled thorns on the thistle. He sighted on a burdock stalk, a hundred yards away, and saw that plainly. With Red padding behind him, Danny left the porch and went into the beech forest.

He stopped, thrust a finger into his mouth to wet it,

and held his wet finger straight up. The wind was steady from the north, with no little cross-currents or eddies to fling scent about. Danny pondered. The snow had stopped falling at about three o'clock in the morning. It hadn't been an unusually severe storm here in the sheltered valleys, but the wind must have blown hard on the tops of the mountains. Therefore, the deer would be down from the wind-blasted heights to the calm valleys, and even if they had gone back their tracks in the snow would be evidence of their going.

Danny called Red to heel, and with the rifle held ready for action at split-second notice, started hunting straight into the wind. Far off a rifle cracked, and its rolling echoes searched the forest as some other early venturing hunter got his shot at a buck. He shot again, and again, while Danny counted. Probably he had jumped the buck and it had run. Very probably it was still running. Danny grinned and thought of the old deer hunter's adage, "One shot, one deer. Two shots, maybe one deer. Three shots, no deer."

Just ahead, a small grove of hemlocks waved their green, needle-tipped branches in the shadow of the towering beeches. Danny walked very softly, and cut around to one side to get a clear view of the open forest there. Nothing moved. There was no sound. Danny bent to enter the hemlocks.

Two deer had bedded beneath them. The snow was melted and packed where they had lain and two separate lines of tracks led away from the beds. Danny followed them until he came to where they left a clear imprint in the deep, soft snow. One of the tracks was very small, the other was the oval, tapered imprint of a doe's hoof.

"Doe and a late fawn," Danny murmured to Red. "We needn't follow 'em."

With Red padding patiently behind him, Danny went deeper into the beech woods. He passed more fresh tracks cutting across the valley, but none that he could positively identify as that of a buck. It was that way sometimes; good hunting country would be overrun by does and fawns.

From time to time the sound of a rifle shot rolled across the beech woods and died in rumbling echoes. The sun climbed high, and strove to burn through the light clouds that were dusted across the sky. Danny stopped and brushed the snow from the end of a moss-covered log. He sat down to eat one of the sandwiches he had brought along. Red crouched in the snow, and gobbled the crusts Danny tossed him.

Danny rose and stood on the log to take a bearing. He had travelled very slowly, averaging about a mile and a half an hour. But he had hunted straight into the unvarying north wind, and was six miles deep in the beech woods. He would hunt in this direction for another hour, then swing up the side of a mountain and quarter back. If the bucks weren't in the beech woods, they had to be in the thickets.

Ten minutes later he found a buck's track, huge, blunted hoof-prints that led straight into the wind. Danny stopped to study the forest ahead, and saw nothing. But the track was very fresh; the buck had come this way not more than twenty minutes ago. If he hunted right he should get a shot within another half hour.

Danny followed the track slowly, feeling for dead, noisy twigs or branches that might lie underneath the snow, before putting a foot down. His thumb was on the hammer of his rifle, ready to pull it back and shoot instantly. His eyes strayed from the buck's trail to the forest ahead, and back to the trail. Ross had taught him long ago that a man who hoped to be a woodsman must read the sign of the woods, and the sign was very plain.

The buck was idling, walking along sure of himself and his safety. But plainly written in the trail he had made was positive evidence that he was old and wise. He avoided all open places, and kept close to the massive trunks of the beeches. He walked from one to the other, keeping as much cover as possible between himself and any possible pursuer. The north wind was strong, and the buck was relying on his nose to inform him of anything that might lie ahead.

Danny came to a place where he had stopped, pawed the snow aside with his front hoofs, and dug in the beech leaves beneath it for the tiny beech nuts that had fallen there. The buck had leaped from his feeding place— there was twenty feet between that and his next track —and had run for a hundred feet more. Then he had stopped to listen.

But he had swung around to face the east, not the south. Danny crouched in his tracks, and tried to visualize exactly what the deer he was following had seen and heard to make him stop here. His gaze roved through the beech forest, and lighted on a dead tree two hundred feet away. A branch leaned from its parent trunk into the snow, and there were tiny scuffings all about where snow had fallen from it. Danny breathed with relief. The buck had merely heard the dead branch fall, and taken momentary alarm.

But now he had swung away from the valley and up the side of the mountain that flanked it. Danny followed, moving even more carefully and slowly because bushes grew among the beeches here. He must be very close to the buck, and a single mis-step or fumble would send it leaping away. Here and there the buck had paused to snatch a mouthful of leaves.

Then he had gone straight toward the rim of a gulley, and the tracks he left were smoking hot. Danny crouched, and travelled swiftly while his heart pounded within him. He knew the gulley, a deep one with only massive trees in it. From either side, anything moving on the other side could be seen. If the buck went into the bottom of the gulley, and up the other side, he would offer a very good shot. If he merely went a little way over the rim and travelled along this side, Danny could follow on top and get a shot anyway. The big buck had made a mistake.

Danny came to the rim of the gulley and slunk behind a tree. He looked down, and slowly raised his rifle. Forty yards below him, in the bottom of the gulley, a doe stood broadside. She was looking back over her shoulder, as though expecting something else to appear.

Two more does stepped from behind a tree, and the head and shoulders of a fourth showed. A hundred and fifty yards up the gulley, another deer appeared. Danny looked hard at it. But it was only another doe, a straggler following this herd.

Then, finally, he saw the buck. It had gone down into and across the gulley, and stood beside a huge beech. So perfectly did its gray coat blend with the gray of the tree that until now it had been almost invisible.

"Don't murder it," Danny breathed to himself. "Give it a chance. Pappy would."

His booted foot strayed to a dead twig lying beside the tree, and crunched down on it. The buck's white tail went up, and as though he had been shot from a catapult he sprang away from the tree. The does stared stupidly at him, and Danny swung his rifle.

The buck was running through the trees, straight up the other side of the gulley. Danny followed him with his pointing gun, and when the buck came into a small open space he squeezed the trigger. An invisible lance seemed to flick forth, and the buck fell so heavily that a little spray of snow leaped into the air. In blind panic the suddenly aroused does began to race away. Danny stood poised, scarcely noticing them, ready to give the buck a second shot should that be necessary. But the big buck lay still.

Danny started happily down the side of the gulley toward his fallen prize. Red plunged after him, but drew back and yelped in sudden excitement. Danny halted.

There was another deer in the gulley, the straggling

doe that had been following the herd. In great, unnaturally long leaps she came pounding straight down the gulley. She jumped very high to clear a fallen log, fell heavily on the other side of it, and did not arise. A muted, sobbing bawl rolled from her throat.

Danny walked wonderingly down to the fallen doe. Blood stained her flanks, and a bullet hole gaped openly there. That, then, was the reason why she had straggled behind the rest. Some pot-hunter had seen something move, and shot without waiting to see whether it bore horns or not. The stricken doe rolled agonized eyes, and Danny shot her through the head.

He knelt beside her with his knife, and pulled off the cockle-burrs that were matted in her white belly hair. It was a case now for John Bailey, the Wintapi warden, though of course Danny would dress the doe so she wouldn't bloat. That done, he found his buck and dragged it into the gulley. He had just finished dressing it when Red growled.

"Nice shooting, kid," a voice said, "darn nice shooting."

Danny whirled and rose with the knife in his hand. The wind was still blowing strongly from the north, and the soft snow was almost noiseless. Even Red hadn't scented the man who had come down the gulley in the wake of the little herd of deer. He was a stocky man, with a hard, wind-reddened face and wearing hunter's clothing. But he flipped the lapel of his coat aside and Danny saw a silver warden's badge gleaming on his shirt.

Red wagged forward to meet him, and rubbed against his woollen trousers. The man reached down to brush a hand across Red's back, and straightened to look at Danny. He grinned, but there was a crooked twist to his lips and a hard, cold something in his eye.

"Nice looking dog, kid," he said casually. "Do you use him to track down the deer you get?"

"That dog don't hunt deer!" Danny flared.

"Well, you do. And that doe will cost you just one hundred dollars."

Danny settled down beside the buck and looked dully at it. A hundred dollars was a big sum, as much as Mr. Haggin paid him in two months for taking care of Red, as much as he and Ross together earned in six weeks on the trap-line. He looked up at the man.

"Look," he said desperately. "I picked this buck's track up back in the beech woods, and tracked him to here. He got in with this mess of does, and I laid him over when he run up the hill. The last doe run down the gulley, tried to jump that log right there, and fell. She couldn't get up again. A pot-hunter had shot her, and all I did was put her out of her pain. That's the honest story, mister."

The warden laughed. "Oh sure. I believe you. But I've been sitting on top of that ridge since daylight, waiting to catch somebody like you, and I don't like sitting that long for nothing. Are you ready to go in?"

Danny said grimly, "I'll go in. But I want to see John Bailey before I pay you anything."

"John Bailey can't do anything for you."

"I'll go in," Danny repeated stubbornly. "If John Bailey thinks I shot that doe, I'll pay. But not otherwise."

The warden grinned sympathetically. "You're in a mess, kid. But I'll give you a break. Give me fifty dollars and I'll forget the whole thing."

"Do you think I'd bring fifty dollars on a deer hunt?"

"Your rifle's worth fifty."

Red came over to Danny, and sat looking uncertainly into his troubled face. Danny's hand automatically went down to stroke the big dog's back. His probing hands paused a second. Then he looked the other man right in the eye.

"Stealin' warden's badges, and makin' out like you're a warden, is against the law, too."

The warden's eyes suddenly became very, very ugly. He purred, "Are you going to get tough about this, kid?"

"Mebbe. How's things in Downdale?"

Danny's glare answered that in the red-cheeked man's face. He watched the other man raise his rifle, cock it, and train it on Danny's heart.

Danny said slowly, "I'd probably be scared of that thing—if it was loaded. You *are* from Downdale, aren't you? And you haven't been sittin' on top of the mountain. You came from Huntz Valley this mornin'. You're aimin' to head deep into the woods, and you got to have grub. You shot the doe in or near Huntz Valley, wounded her, and couldn't shoot again on account of you was out of ammunition. You followed her here, hopin' she'd fall . . ."

The red-faced man lunged forward. Danny brought his own rifle up, squeezed the trigger, and watched the bullet plow a long white furrow in the stock of the other man's gun. Splinters flew, and a little trickle of blood started down the other's wrist. Danny backed away, but his gun was ready.

"Don't try it again," he warned. "I didn't miss because I couldn't hit. We're goin' for a walk, but you're walkin' ahead."

It was mid-afternoon when they reached the cabin in the beech woods, and Danny ushered his prisoner inside. He handed the rifle to Ross.

"Watch him, Pappy," he said. "Don't let him get away."

"What's up, Danny?"

"Escaped prisoner. I'll be back."

Ross said grimly, "He'll be here when you get back."

With Red beside him, Danny went back into the snow and down the trail to Mr. Haggin's Wintapi estate. Mr. Haggin had gone south for the winter. But there were caretakers there, and they had telephones. Danny gave the three long rings that called John Bailey, and listened until he heard the warden's voice.

"Hello."

"Hello. This is Danny Pickett. Did one of your new deputies get in a ruckus, and lose his badge?"

"Why, why . . . Where are you, Danny?"

"At Mr. Haggin's."

"I'll be right up. Wait."

Twenty minutes later John Bailey drove into the yard,

and Danny went out to meet him. The tall warden got out of his car, and stood with one foot on the running board. Red came forward. John Bailey stooped to pat his head, and looked at Danny.

"You had it right," he said seriously. "I was warned two days ago that an escaped convict from Downdale was thought to be hiding in here. This morning Ike Lowman was slugged over near Huntz Valley, and his badge and rifle taken. But the rifle had only one cartridge in the chamber. We couldn't track because there must have been fifty hunters went up that side of the mountain this morning. But the hunt is organized, and I've been trying to get more men out by telephone—that's how come you caught me at home. Now what about it?" he demanded.

"We got your man."

"Where is he?"

"Sittin' up in the house. Pappy's holdin' a gun on him."

John Bailey whistled. "How the dickens did you catch him?"

"I read the sign," Danny said. "I shot a buck this mornin', 'way back in the beech woods. A wounded doe fell a little way from it, and I shot her. Then this man came along with a warden's badge, and at first I thought he was a warden. When he said he'd forget the fine if I gave him fifty dollars, I suspicioned he wasn't. When he said he'd take my gun instead of the fifty, I knew he wasn't. I knew the doe had come from Huntz Valley. When I found out this man had come from there too, and hadn't been sittin' on top of the mountain like he told me, it was easy to figure the rest."

"How did you find out?"

"From Red," Danny said softly. "There's eight miles of beech woods between where I shot that buck and Huntz Valley, and there ain't a thing but trees among 'em. That doe had cockle-burrs stuck in her hair, so I knew she'd come from Huntz Valley on account of that's the only place where any cockle-burrs grow. I didn't even think to look for any on the man. But I combed Red clean last night. He rubbed against this man's pants, and when he came back to me there was cockle-burrs in *his* hair, too.

"Come on up and get your man, Mr. Bailey. But you'll have to bring him back alone. Pappy's sick and I got work to do. There's two deer in the beech woods, and I got to take Asa and bring 'em out."

CHAPTER 9

TRAP-LINE PIRATE

IT WAS DARK WHEN DANNY LED ASA OUT OF THE BEECH woods and up to the maple tree in the pasture. The doe and buck were dragging behind the mule, sliding like sleds over the soft snow. Danny hung them in the tree, and for a moment stood with one hand on the buck's frozen carcass. A warm feeling crept through him. Life in the beech woods might be hard, harsh, and dangerous. But only the strong survived there, and Danny felt a swelling pride as that fact was driven home to him. The dead buck, hung by its antlers and swinging gently in the wind, was more than just another deer. It was another achievement and another victory, an assurance that he was strong. Danny stabled and fed Asa, and went into the cabin.

Ross was sitting in front of the stove, and Danny's hot supper simmered on it. Red threw himself down on his bed. Danny felt like doing the same. But a man just couldn't give way to weariness. He sat down to eat the meal his father had prepared, and leaned back to sigh.

"Hard day?" Ross inquired.

Danny shrugged. "There was a lot to do."

Neither spoke any more of the day's incidents. What was past was done with. What lay ahead was important. Ross drank a glass of water and coughed. Danny looked at him.

"How you feelin'?"

"Better. I'll be all set in a couple more days. It's hard to sit in, but I reckon it was a foolishness to want to get out."

"It sure was. And I'm glad you're seein' it that way."

"You aimin' to run Stoney Lonesome, come mornin'?"

"Yup."

"All of it?"

Danny hesitated. Stoney Lonesome was a long line. When travel was good, and unencumbered by snow, it was possible to leave the shanty in the beech woods at half-past two in the morning, go to the end of the Stoney Lonesome line, and be back by dark. But with snow on the ground, Stoney Lonesome was a two-day line. Danny looked keenly at Ross.

"That depends on how you're feelin'."

"I'm all right," Ross said. "I can take care of Asa and the milkin'."

"You sure?"

"Certain sure," Ross grinned. "Don't be such a fuss-budget."

"Well, I reckon I might as well run all of it."

"You might as well. I'll make you a pack."

When dawn came, Danny was far up the mountain. He swung the pack on his shoulders a little to one side, and shifted the axe that hung from his belt so that its wooden handle would not continue to rub the same place on his hip. He brought one narrow-webbed snowshoe up beside the other and turned to look back at Red.

"How do you like winter in the Wintapi, Red? It sure enough is here!"

The big red setter, walking where Danny had packed the snow and stepping over the intervening ridges, came up and sat down on the tail ends of Danny's snowshoes. He raised his head and wagged his plumed tail gently back and forth as Danny slipped one mitten off and reached down to tickle his ears. Danny looked over the dog, down into the valley that yawned below him, at the winter-stripped beech trees that rattled gauntly in the wind. It was cold, but not so cold that the foxes wouldn't be running or the little white ermine sneaking through the thickets in their eternal quest for something to kill. A worried little frown creased Danny's brow. The cabin in the beech woods was three hours' snow-shoeing from this point . . . But Ross would be all right.

Danny stooped to pry the ice out of his snowshoe harness, and one by one lifted the paws of the red setter to dig out any ice that might have collected on them. He was proud of Red. You took a hound along on a trap-line and the first thing you knew he was stealing bait, or leaving his scent around a fox trap, or blundering into a trap and howling to be let out. But it had taken only two days to teach Red all about traps.

Of course a dog wasn't much help on a trap-line. But it was a lot of comfort to have company up here, and a man never could tell what might happen when he was out this way.

Danny thought again of Ross, back in the cabin, and a little grin played about his lips. Danny himself had set most of the traps on Stoney Lonesome, and so far they had taken most of the fur that Ross had brought in. But, so far, Ross had run the line and re-set sprung traps. This time, if Danny could re-set sprung traps himself, and take a heavy catch of fur when they ran the line again, he would have a lot to say as to who was the real trapper of the family. The friendly rivalry between him-self and Ross had existed for seven years now, ever since, as a boy of ten, Danny had first gone out on the long trap-lines.

"Dog," he said with mock severity, "if you'll heave

yourself off my webs, we'll get on. It's a smart ways to the end of this here line and we won't hit the line cabin before dark, come what may."

Danny resumed his journey up the ridge, bending his head against the gale that roared down it. Waiting until he got under way, and again stepping carefully in his snowshoe tracks, Red followed. A snowshoe rabbit hopped across the trail in front of him, and Danny thought wistfully of the .22 rifle he had left back in the cabin. But he had enough to eat and every ounce of weight counted on the trap-line. If a man picked up a heavy load of foxes to be pelted he had enough to carry.

The trail cut sharply upward, along the side of a shallow gulley that sloped from the top of Stoney Lonesome. Danny saw a jack pine beside the trail with three blazes in its gnarled trunk. He stooped, and shaded his eyes with his hands while he peered across the gulley at an unfreezing spring where there was a water set for fox. Nothing had disturbed the trap. With Red padding behind him, he resumed his journey and broke over the top of the mountain.

The character of the country changed abruptly. The valleys were laden with massive beech trees. Farther up, the mountain sides supported groves of aspen and an occasional jack pine. But here, on top, a veritable jungle of twisted laurel covered everything. Only an occasional pine reared above it, and the only way through was on the path that Danny and Ross kept open. But the laurel was the abode of numberless rabbits, both cottontail and snowshoe. Foxes and weasels had gathered to live on the rabbits, and an occasional marten or fisher drifted through. Useless for any other purpose, the top of Stoney Lonesome was a trapper's paradise.

Danny started snowshoeing along the twisted, snake-like trail. Presently, twenty feet ahead, he saw another of the triple-blazed trees that marked a trap in the brush. Red plunged around and ahead of him, wallowing chest-deep through the piled snow. Suddenly the dog's tail stiffened, and a snarl rippled from his throat.

Danny slipped a mitten from his hand, and let it dangle from the string around his neck. He drew the belt axe from its sheath, and with that in his hand crept forward. Carefully, the axe poised, he went into the brush and came to the set. Another snarl gurgled from Red's throat, and the big red dog edged around Danny to stand with his tail stiff and his hackles raised.

Danny paused, the axe held high, while his eyes darted around the brush and back to the fox set. The two traps that composed it had been carefully buried in the snow, and covered with tissue paper so they would not freeze. The bait, a scented bit of snowshoe rabbit, had hung over the set. But now, for ten feet around, the snow was beaten down and stained with blood. Bits of red fur and particles of flesh were scattered about. The two traps hung over a bush, and from them dangled the ripped carcass of what had been a fine red fox. Danny advanced, knelt beside the fox, and examined it closely. Its pelt was torn beyond hope of repair, and even half of its red tail had been bitten off. A rank, musty odor defiled the air and the traps had been scored by sharp teeth. Danny twirled the axe in his hand, and spoke softly to the dog.

"Injun devil!"

With his hands he pressed down the springs of the two traps, let the fox slide from them into the snow, and put the traps in his pack. Not often did an Indian devil, or wolverene, invade the Wintapi. But when one did, and found a trap-line, the unfortunate trapper had either to kill the pirate or pull his traps. Danny looked angrily across the laurel, and spoke again to the dog.

"Injun devil, by criminey!"

It was bad, very bad. Four years ago another wolverene had come into the Wintapi and established a run on two lines of Ross Pickett's fox traps. Ross had set for it every trap that a lifetime spent in the woods had revealed to him. But still the Indian devil had triumphed. That year Ross and Danny had taken less than half their normal catch of fur, and summer had brought lean times to the cabin in the beech woods.

Red stalked forward, plowing through the deep snow. He stopped beside a laurel bush, whined softly, and waited for Danny to advance to his side. The wolverene had left the ruined set here, and the broad trail plowed by its stubby body was plain where it had gone into the laurel. Danny looked speculatively back toward the cabin in the beech woods. His father's hounds, taking a trail so fresh, might bay their quarry. But it would take three hours to get the hounds, and three more to bring them back here. Nothing was more diabolically cunning than a wolverene. If the hounds took a trail six hours old, they would stand little chance of overtaking the Indian devil. Besides, there were the rest of the traps to think of. This was the wolverene's first appearance on the line. He might not have found all the traps. The thing to do was make the rounds, take any good pelts that were in the traps, then come back with the hounds to try and hunt the wolverene down.

Danny snowshoed back to the trail, and set off down it at a fast pace. For a little space Red crowded ahead to plunge through the deep snow beside him, and Danny let his mittened hand trail along the red setter's back. But the going was too rough; Red dropped back again to walk where Danny's snowshoes had packed the trail.

A quarter of a mile farther on was the next set, which had caught nothing. But sprung and empty, the two traps lay on top of the snow where the wolverene had left them after it had contemptuously scratched particles of ice and snow over them to spring them. Danny's eyes were cloudy, and little angry flecks washed back and forth in them as he examined the trail where the Indian devil had again disappeared into the laurel. The wolverene was not only on a trap-line, but he knew that he was and apparently was determined to find and defile or spoil every trap on it. Danny left the traps where they lay, and took the axe from its sheath to swing it in his hand.

"Damn him!" he gritted. "Damn his ugly hide!"

A fresh burst of wind, casting whirling flakes of snow before it, roared across the flat top of Stoney Lonesome. Danny blinked, and bent his head as he plodded forward. Ross, if he was here, would probably have some idea of what to do with an Indian devil on the rampage. But Ross was not here, and whatever was to be done Danny had to do. The dangling chain of one of the traps in his pack caught on a bush and fell to the snow. Danny retraced his steps to pick the trap up, and Red brushed against his knees. Another almost inaudible growl bubbled from the dog's throat as Danny swerved from the trail to the next set.

Again Red lunged ahead of him, plowing through the snow and snarling. Danny ran on his snowshoes, the axe in his hand raised and ready to strike. He saw the trapped fox, a shining bit of red-gold, crouched flat in the snow and staring fixedly into the laurel. Red stopped. His body stiffened. His hackles raised, and for a moment he stood on point. Then a great, thunderous battle challenge rolled from his throat and he lunged forward again. Danny made a wild swing with his free hand, and slipped his mittened fingers through Red's collar.

Red fought his restraining hand, and snarled almost continuously as he strained toward the laurel. Danny stopped, trying with his eyes to pierce the almost impenetrable brush. But all he could see was the laurel. He spoke to the raging dog.

"Easy. Take it easy, Red."

Red quieted, but stood trembling and tense. Slowly, a step at a time, they went forward. There was a momentary lull in the wind, and Danny snapped his head erect. Behind him, a sudden rattle of steel sounded as the fox in the trap leaped sideways. Then, twenty feet away, the brush rattled. Red snarled, and for a moment struggled to be free. Danny settled slowly down on his snowshoes, and again tried to peer through the matted tangle of laurel stems.

At first he could see nothing. Then, among the boulders and snow-covered ends of logs that were scattered through the laurel, he caught the dark sheen of fur. Danny fixed his gaze on it, and very slowly the head and fore-quarters of the marauding wolverene assumed distinct outline. It stood beside a log, its front paws on a rock, staring steadily at him. Then as suddenly and silently as it had come, it was gone.

Red strove forward, but Danny pulled him back. A little shiver travelled up and down his spine, and an icy hand seemed to clutch the back of his neck. Not for nothing had trappers who encountered them considered the wolverene as the incarnation of everything evil. There had been evil in its attitude, hate in its steady stare. Danny shivered again.

"Come on," he murmured to Red. "That thing would kill you quicker'n you could kill a mouse. We got to get that fox."

Once on the trail again, Danny unbuckled Red's collar, slipped it through the ring on the end of a trap chain, and put it back on the dog. He looked back down the trail, toward the cabin in the beeches, and again wished mightily that Ross was here to guide him. He had no weapons with which he might successfully fight a wolverene. But when a man didn't have what he wanted, it was his place to make the best use of what he had. Of one thing he was certain; Red must not be allowed to go into the brush and fight the wolverene. If he did he would be killed.

Danny looked up the trail toward the overnight cabin at the end of the trap-line. There might be more pelts in some of the traps, and if he did not get them today the wolverene surely would. Besides, he and Red had never yet been run out of their mountains, not even by the huge Old Majesty. Of course, at least to a dog, a wolverene was much more dangerous than any bear. Most dogs knew enough to keep out of a bear's way, but would not hesitate to close with an Indian devil. But he could keep Red on the chain. Danny started up the trail, holding his hand behind him so Red would have plenty of room to walk in his snowshoe tracks.

Another blast of wind rolled across the mountain top and whirled down the slope. It left more snow in its wake, ice-edged, whirling bits of half sleet that slithered crisply against the green laurel and rattled on Danny's hood. He bent his head, keeping his eyes fixed on the left side of the trail. Ross had certainly known what he was doing when he insisted on marking all sets on one side of the trail. Three blazes meant the trap was on the left, three blazes with a bar on top meant the right. But in a storm like this it was right handy when a man had to look only one way. Danny looked back at his snow-shoe tracks. Ten feet behind, they were already filling with snow. Red bumped his leg, and looked at him through snow-filled eyes. Far off, the wind howled in a shriller key.

The next trap held a brown marten, and hope began to rise in Danny. The wolverene must have come on the trap-line only that morning, and had not found all the traps. Danny thrust the marten into his pack beside the fox, and shouldered it to continue up the trail. He felt better. He had had every reason for leaving the mountain top. But he hadn't left it. Ross would not have left either, and anything Ross would or would not do must be the right thing.

The howling wind abated a little, but the swirling snow fell more thickly. The gray sky had added more layers of color to its overcast self. Danny took another fox from a trap, and passed by half a dozen sets that were still undisturbed. As he passed a huge pine beside the trail, he nodded in satisfaction. Despite the storm, and deep-snow travel, he had made good time. There was one more set between this pine and the cabin, which he should reach shortly after dark. Suddenly, snapping the chain taut and jerking Danny's arm around, Red crowded up beside him.

Now in semi-darkness, the laurel rattled and whispered mournfully as the snow beat against it and the few little breezes that had not kept pace with the gale whispered through it. Red stood beside the trail, hackles bristled and lips raised. Another snarl came from his throat. Danny knelt beside him, and stroked the dog's ear with his mitten.

"Don't go off half-cocked," he murmured. "Easy, Red."

Red crowded very close to him, whimpering softly,

while Danny reached down to unfasten the snap cover
of his axe sheath. The wolverene had not deserted the
trap-line, then, but had circled it to come in from the
other end. He was ahead now, possibly waiting and possibly destroying the last trap. Danny reached out to encircle the dog's neck with his arm. If it came to a fight, he
and Red would fight together. But Red must not be allowed to go into the brush alone. In the gathering darkness, the laurel jungle seemed almost a solid mass on
either side of the shimmering white trail.

Danny glanced back toward the big pine, but its top
was invisible against the night sky. With his left hand,
he took a firmer grip on the trap attached to Red's collar, and with the belt axe in his right began to snowshoe
up the trail. Red walked beside him, still tense and alert
as he plowed through the deep snow. He stopped, and
strained toward the brush, while again the thunderous
battle challenge rumbled from his throat.

Danny paused for a fraction of a second while some
cold sixth sense functioned within him. He knew that
the wolverene was there, very close, and that its intended prey this time was no helpless trapped creature
but himself and Red. Danny began to run, racing up
the trail, half-dragging Red with him. He saw the dark
mass of the overnight cabin looming ahead. Danny
pulled the latch string and opened the door.

He stumbled into the cabin, slammed the door behind him, and leaned, panting, against it. He dropped
the trap that was attached to Red's collar, and heard the
dog dragging it across the floor.

After a few seconds Danny took off his mittens and stooped in the darkness to unlace his snowshoe harnesses. He stepped out of them, and reached into his pocket for the box of water-proof matches that he carried wherever he went. Striking one on the side of the box, he stepped to the table and touched the flaming match to the wick of a candle that stood upright in the neck of a syrup bottle. The candle's glare revealed in dull yellow outline every nook and corner of the cabin.

It was an eight by ten shack, with a bunk at one end and a fireplace, built of stone gathered on Stoney Lonesome, filling the other. A few simple cooking utensils hung on wooden pegs driven into the wall beside the fireplace, and folded blankets were piled at one end of the bunk. The cabin had never been intended for anything except a sleeping place when either Ross or Danny might be at this end of the Stoney Lonesome trap-line.

Danny felt for the axe at his belt, and with a shock discovered that it was gone. It had been in his hand at the last place Red had scented the wolverene. He must have dropped it during the ensuing wild flight. Danny clenched his hands. A trapper did not necessarily have to have a gun, but an axe was almost indispensable. Well, he would have to get along without one tonight. There was a stack of wood piled beside the door. He could bring in an arm load, shave kindling sticks with his skinning knife, and have a fire. Usually they left kindling sticks in the cabin. But the last time, for some reason, they had been overlooked.

Red padded over to him. Danny unbuckled his collar, slipped the dragging trap from it, and put the collar back on. Snow rattled crisply against the sod-thatched roof, and outside the angry wind was again shrieking its rage. Danny set a pan before the candle, so it would not blow out when the door was opened, and turned to lift the latch. The candle flickered slightly, and a dull thud sounded as the wind blew a loose branch or stub against the side of the cabin. Then Red trotted to the center of the floor and stood looking at the roof. A low growl rolled from him. Danny took his hand from the latch and backed against the door.

The wind was attacking in short, angry charges that blasted the cabin and staggered, spent, from it. But during its split second lulls there was another and very distinct sound. Something that was neither wind clawing at the thatch nor hard snow rattling against it, scraped on the roof. Danny listened, open-mouthed. He felt sweat start from his temples and roll down his face. His throat tightened. The wolverene was on the roof, trying to claw a hole through it.

Danny moved from the door to the center of the hut. His eyes roved about it, alighting in turn on each of the objects it held. He lifted the coffee pot, and balanced it in his hand. A few bits of frozen dirt sifted through the poles that supported the thatch. Danny swung the coffee pot in a long arc. It was a poor weapon, but better than his short-bladed skinning knife.

He licked his dry lips, and knelt beside Red with his hand on the dog's ruff. Both their glances strayed to the roof. Danny clenched his free hand. Even bears feared wolverenes, and if this one got into the cabin . . . But Ross had always said that if a man didn't have what he needed, he could make out some way with what he had. Danny fumbled in his pack, and moved away from Red, toward the fireplace.

Abruptly, the scraping on the roof ceased. There was the sound of something moving across it, and a second's silence. Red sprang forward, and Danny warned him away.

"Stay back! Back here!"

Red stopped. The pan that sheltered the candle fell down, and the candle's glow again filled the room. Bits of soot and dirt tumbled into the fireplace, and Danny stared in terrified fascination at the wide chimney. There was a little thud, and the wolverene tumbled from the chimney into the open fireplace, to stand blinking. In one mighty leap Red bridged the distance between them and closed. Danny felt the trip-hammer beat of his own heart as he ran forward with the coffee pot poised.

He danced on the balls of his feet beside the fighting pair, awaiting a chance to strike. But they were rolling over and over on the floor, and Danny's heart seemed to stop beating as he saw the wolverene's powerful jaws fastened in Red's chest. He stooped, and with a wild stab grasped one of the wolverene's back paws. The other plowed a bloody row of furrows down his arm. Danny jerked, and the wolverene arched his body to bring his jaws back and snap. His slashing teeth closed on Danny's trousers, and Danny kicked hard as the fighting beast fell to the floor with a strip of wool cloth in his mouth. The wolverene's foul musk filled the cabin. Danny stumbled, as a little clod of chinking fell to the floor beside him.

Almost at once he was on his feet again, back to the wall. Red had not known how to fight a wolverene when he started to fight this one. But he knew now. The big setter had dived in, closed his teeth on the side of the wolverene's neck, and was straining backward. The wolverene's rage bubbled through his constricted wind pipe, as he strove to bring his back claws into play. But Red had learned the deadly danger of those claws, and whirled aside whenever they struck. The big setter's jaws ground deeper.

Danny watched the wolverene try frantically to rip the dog apart with his front claws. But they were encased in the only weapons Danny had had with which he might have any chance of fighting this thing successfully—the two steel fox traps he had picked up and set before the fireplace when he heard the wolverene coming down it. The wolverene's breath came in wheezing gasps, and Red dived in to take a firmer hold.

*   *   *

Late the next afternoon, carrying Red across his shoulders on top of his pack, Danny stumbled into the cabin in the beech woods. He put the dog in his bed by the stove, took off his snowshoes, and slipped out of his coat. Ross, who knew from long experience the many things that could happen on a trap-line, waited for him to speak.

"He got clawed up some, Pappy. But he's all right. Mr. Haggin can even show him at another dog show if he wants. I packed him the last four miles because he was lame."

He took the two foxes and the marten pelt from his pack. "We got these," he said.

For a moment he stood over the pack, looking from it to the injured dog. Then, because it would not do for a trapper to boast, he lifted the last pelt out quietly.

"There was an Injun devil too, Pappy. He messed up the traps some. But we got him. Red and me got him."

CHAPTER 10

SHEILAH MACGUIRE

THE WINTER WORE SWIFTLY ON, WITH JANUARY BRINGING its cold and February great, feathery drifts of snow. Ross and Danny were out every day from before dawn until dark, and the stretched furs in the fur shed reached in a long line from one end to the other, and back again. Ross took his hounds into the mountains, brought back a few wildcat and lynx pelts and the fisher he had marked earlier in the fall.

Late in February Moe Snass, the Wintapi's fur buyer, led his pack mule up the Smokey Creek trail. For hours Moe, Ross, and Danny stood in the cold shed haggling over the value of the pelts that hung there. But Ross grinned, and winked surreptitiously at Danny, when he pocketed the check that, finally and unwillingly, Moe wrote for him. They stood together, watching the fur buyer lead his laden pack mule down the trail. Ross grinned again.

"He paid more'n he wanted to," he observed. "It's been a good year, Danny."

"It sure has. We didn't cheat him, did we, Pappy?"

Ross laughed. "Any time you cheat Moe, you'll see pink owls flyin' 'round in the day-time. Nope. He made himself a nice profit, but not as much as he would of liked."

Red bounded forward and buried his face in the snow, sniffing eagerly at a field mouse in its drift-covered tunnel. He shook the loose snow from his muzzle and came bouncing back to Danny. Ross took the check from his pocket, and looked at it.

"Five hundred and sixty dollars, Danny. And the muskrat and beaver still got to come into their prime. We're like to make two hundred dollars more. Let's jaunt up the valley and look at them six fox traps we got in the beeches."

"Sure thing."

They donned snowshoes and side by side set off

through the beech forest. Red paced behind, stepping in their tracks and looking interestedly about for whatever showed. A fox had walked among the beeches, his dainty trail plain in the new-fallen snow that topped the crust of the old fall. Ross swerved, and the fox leaped wildly away from the trunk of a huge beech to bring up at the end of the trap that held him. He crouched in the snow, his bushy tail curled around his flanks, trying to hide. Ross put his gloved hands on his hips, and turned to Danny.

"This is it, huh?"

"It looks thataway."

Instead of a burnished and gleaming red-gold, the fox's pelt was dully copper. The weather was still cold. But the sun was higher and brighter, and during the day the fox had lain on high ledges to absorb such warmth as it offered. It had bleached his pelt, and thus its value was cut sharply. No trapper who hoped to continue trapping ever killed any fur animal except when it was near peak value. Ross knelt beside the trapped fox, and his gloved hand shot out to seize its neck. His other hand closed over its slim jaws, and Danny removed the trap from its paw. The liberated fox sped away among the trees, and Ross grinned after it.

"He'll be there for next year. I reckon we pull our fox traps, Danny."

"I reckon we do."

"We may as well start with these six."

They picked up the six fox traps and carried them down to store in the shed. The next day they made the long trip over half of Stoney Lonesome, taking one good fox and liberating two that, like the one in the valley, had been burned. Red pranced ahead of them, burying his face in the snow and then playfully shaking it off. When they reached the valley he dashed with puppyish enthusiasm at a black crow that clung forlornly to a dead branch. Ross grinned.

"It's sure enough time to pull fox traps. The first robin won't be more'n three weeks behind the first crow."

"That's right," Danny agreed. "Say, Pappy, there's a good bit of daylight left. If you can pack these traps in, I can swing up the valley and see if the beaver are movin' in that pond by the aspens."

"We'll get our share even if they ain't," Ross grunted. "But go ahead anyhow."

With the heavy pack on his shoulders Ross swung down through the beech woods toward the cabin. Happiness, somehow tempered by doubt, went with him. Spring was not far off, and with it Mr. Haggin would come back to his big estate. And Mr. Haggin, though he had made no definite promises, had certainly hinted that he was going to take Danny in hand and teach him all about dogs.

Ross could not help the doubt. Never in his life had anyone given him anything, nor had he ever had anything at all for which he had not traded hard and often bitter physical toil. But Danny was different. Danny was like his mother, and it was in him to be more than just a trapper. Fervently Ross hoped that Mr. Haggin lived up to his unspoken promises. Danny was happy enough with Red. But there were so many horizons of which Ross, as a life-long trapper, had had only a bare and tantalizing glimpse, and that might open completely for Danny if only things worked out right.

"I hope they do," Ross murmured to himself. "I hope, Mr. Haggin, that you take that boy in hand. You won't be sad if you do."

He left the traps in the shed, entered the cabin, and started a fire. He was in the midst of preparing supper when there was a knock at the door. Ross opened it to confront Curley Jordan, one of the caretakers from Mr. Haggin's estate. Curley thrust a yellow envelope at him.

"What is it?" Ross inquired.

"Telegram," Curley said.

Ross opened it, read it, thanked Curley, and shut the door in his face. Then he retreated to the darkest corner of the cabin to sit down on a chair with his chin in his hands. His forehead creased, and he stared moodily at the floor. He had always known that some day such a thing was inevitable. But Danny was so young! Not even eighteen!

Ross picked the telegram up, re-read it, and rose to pace the floor. But when he heard Danny take his snowshoes off and hang them beside the door he hastily shoved the telegram under the bread box. Danny burst in, his cheeks flushed and his eyes bright. Red padded in behind him and wagged over to greet Ross, who was puttering unconcernedly about the table.

"How's it out?" Ross said over his shoulder.

"Breakin'. The pussy-willow stalks are plumb green,

and there's an inch of water over the ice on the beaver dam. Two more weeks of winter is the most we'll get."

"Yeh?"

Ross absently tossed a paring knife into the air and caught it by the handle. His brow wrinkled in perplexity. This wasn't something a man could bull or bluff his way through. Young people were pretty sensitive about their business, and apt to get huffy if somebody tried to run it for them. It was a time for subtlety. But Ross didn't know how to be subtle.

"Danny," he said bluntly, "do you trust me?"

"Why, why sure, Pappy."

"All right. I don't aim to mind your business for you. But if there's any way I can help you, I will."

"What you talkin' about?"

"I'm talkin' about this woman you met when you took Red to the dog show in New York! Danny, she's comin' here!"

"What!"

"Here it is," Ross insisted. He took the telegram from beneath the bread box and thrust it at Danny. "Read it yourself. I expect you to do whatever's right. But if this Haggin's aimin' to palm off one of his female relatives on a boy what don't know his own mind I'll . . ."

"Wait a minute." Danny opened the telegram and read, "MEET SHEILAH MACGUIRE ON 10 PM TRAIN AT WINTAPI STATION. REGARDS. HAGGIN." He folded the telegram and stared over it. Then he began to laugh. "Pappy, that's no woman. It's a dog!"

"A huh?"

"A dog!" Danny repeated. "A mate for Red. Mr. Haggin said he'd send one up just as soon as he got one good enough! Just think, Pappy! We're goin' to raise pups here, good pups, show and field dogs! Man, oh man, Pappy! Just think!"

Ross scratched his head dubiously. "You sure?"

"Of course!" Danny danced around the table. "I was too busy at the dog show to meet any women in New York. Just think of the pups we're goin' to have, Pappy! Two years from now I bet one of 'em takes first in show at Madison Square! We'll have to keep her warm and everything, Pappy! And . . ."

"Sheilah MacGuire!" Ross snorted. "Who ever heard of a dog named that? Mebbe-so, if the cabin ain't comfortable enough for her, we can build a steam-heated house!"

"We don't need it," Danny said, blissfully unconscious of the sarcasm. "Let's see now, spring pups make awful good ones. By gosh, I can take a couple of 'em this fall and start 'em huntin' with Red. What time is it, Pappy?"

"Twenty to five."

"Whew! I better go!"

"You better," Ross said drily. "It's four whole miles to the Wintapi station, and you ain't got but five hours and twenty minutes to make it."

Nevertheless, Danny insisted on leaving at once, and when Red would have followed he ordered him back. The big dog went to his blanket beside Danny's bed, and looked resentfully out of his brown eyes. Ross snapped his fingers, and Red padded defiantly over to sit beside him. Ross addressed him with mock sympathy.

"I hope you got your wild oats all planted, Red. There's a woman comin' into your life."

From the doorway, Danny grinned. He left the cabin, strapped on his snowshoes, and started up the long valley that led over a mountain to the Wintapi station. A happy little song trailed from his lips as he travelled, and his feet seemed to bear wings. His brightest and most hopeful dreams were at last coming true; he was going to raise fine dogs. Maybe Sheilah MacGuire would bear a big litter, and all would be champions. Danny grinned ruefully. Maybe at least *one* would be. Danny snowshoed down to the Wintapi station, and for two hours shivered in the late-winter wind that swept it. He went inside the fireless station, and sat on a porcupine-chewed bench while an endless procession of wonderful red dogs gambolled and frolicked through his mind. Then, at long last, he heard the train whistle.

Danny rushed out to the platform, watched the train stab the darkness with its single headlight, and stamped his feet restlessly as it drew near. As it stopped, the door of the express car rolled open. The agent thrust his head out.

"Hey, are you waitin' for a dog?"

"Yup."

"Here it is."

He thrust a crate through the door, and Danny lowered it excitedly to the ground. His heart pumped crazily. From the brief glimpse he had had through the slatted crate in the car's dim light, the dog within had looked like none other than the setter that most nearly approached Red's perfection, the one that had competed with him for best of breed. But it couldn't be—Mr. Haggin had said that no money could buy her.

The train rushed into the darkness and Danny knelt beside the crate. The dog within whined, and pressed her cold nose against Danny's questing hand. Her wagging tail bumped the side of the crate, and she whined again. A short, sharp bark cut the night's silence, and the dog scratched with her front paw at the gateway of her prison. Danny murmured soothingly.

"Oh, sure, sure, Sheilah. Here's me lookin' at you, and you wantin' to get out. I bet you're tired, cold, and hungry."

He felt about in the darkness, found the wire that held the crate's door shut, and untwisted it. He opened the door, and the dog minced hesitatingly forward. She sat down before Danny, and bent her long, finely formed head upward as she looked at him. Danny stroked her ears, and gently tickled her muzzle. His hands went over her in the darkness, feeling her ribs, her loins, her back, and her rear legs. A sigh escaped him. You could tell almost as much by feeling a dog as you could by looking at one, and if this wasn't Dr. MacGruder's bitch it was an exact replica. Danny took a length of buckskin thong from his pocket, slipped it under the dog's collar, and again spoke to her.

"This is only until we know each other, Sheilah. Right now we can't take a chance of losin' one another in the dark night."

He started up through the forest, retracing the snow-shoe trail he had made coming down, and for a space Sheilah floundered in the snow beside him. Gently but firmly Danny forced her behind, made her walk where his snowshoes had packed the snow. And he travelled slowly. Sheilah was not Red, who knew the tricks and ways of the forest. But she would learn.

Danny swung back down into the beech woods, toward the cabin, and Sheilah plunged and bucked as, for the first time in her life, the smell of wood smoke drifted to her sensitive nostrils. Danny knelt beside her, stroking her smooth sides with his hand and talking quietly. A balmy little breeze, fore-runner of the warmth that was to come, played up the valley and pushed the cold air before it. Danny heard Red's challenging bark. The hounds came out of their kennels and bayed sleepily. Ross stood framed in the open door.

"You got her, Danny?"

"Yeah. I'll fetch her in in a minute."

He knelt beside the trembling dog, stroking her sides and talking gently to her. Irish setters were a special breed in themselves, sensitive, intelligent, and proud. You had to handle them right or you couldn't handle them at all. Doubt or mistrust in their minds was very hard to overcome, and getting off to the right start with a new Irish setter was essential. The dog stopped trembling, laid her head on Danny's thigh, and sighed. For a few moments more he fussed over her.

When he rose, Sheilah walked confidently beside him and stayed very close to his knees while he took off his snowshoes. A little uncertain, but no longer trembling, she walked up the steps and into the cabin. Then her trepidation returned. She shrank against Danny, the being who had released her from the crate, the person who obviously had had most to do with terminating her long and onerous train ride.

"There she is," Danny said proudly.

"Whew!" Ross whistled. "Is that ever a dog! But she's scared, Danny."

"They're all high strung."

"Well, we got to calm her."

Ross dropped a piece of fat beef into the skillet and put it on the stove. It sputtered there, and when it was cooked he carried it over to hold it under the aristocratic nose of Sheilah MacGuire. She sniffed at it, licked it with her tongue, and finally accepted it. She smelled at Ross's trousers, his shirt, his hands, his shoes, etching in her keen mind an indelible picture of this man who, apparently, meant only to be kind and could be trusted. Danny knelt beside her, hand on her shining ruff.

"See how she acts with Red," Ross suggested.

Danny glanced around to see Red sitting before the stove, apparently engaged in a deep study of the cabin's opposite wall. He snapped his fingers.

"Come here, Red. Come over and meet Sheilah."

The big dog rose. Looking only at the open door, haughtily ignoring all other occupants of the cabin, he stalked regally into the night.

Danny stared, dumfounded. Sheilah wriggled a little closer to him, and opened her slender jaws to lick his hand. Danny looked out the open door, then up at Ross.

"What the dickens . . . ?"

"Haw, haw, haw!" Ross sat on a chair, bent double with laughter. He straightened to gasp, "You got him a mate, Danny. But you forgot to ask him if he wanted one!"

"What's the matter with him?"

"He's jealous, you loon! He's been king-pin 'round here long's he's been here. Now you got another dog to pet. That's what's eatin' him."

"Well, I'll be darned!"

Danny's gaze strayed from the slight Sheilah to the open door, and back again. He had known that Red would want to be boss of his own household, and that Sheilah would do as he thought best. But it never occurred to him that Red wouldn't even want a mate.

"What'll I do?" he appealed.

"I dunno." Ross shook his head lugubriously, but laughter still sparkled in his eyes. "Mebbe," he suggested helpfully, "you could write to one of these here newspaper people who give advice to all romantical things and . . ."

"I'm not foolin', Pappy."

"He'll come back if you kick her out."

"She'll run away."

"Likely she will," Ross agreed gravely, "but she sure ain't goin' to share Red's bed. Given she's in here at all, she can have all of it."

"Watch her," Danny said decisively. "I'm goin' out and see if I can argue with that old fool."

He took a flashlight and went outside. The yard about was tracked up, by both men and dogs, and there was no possibility of choosing Red's trail from among so many. Mike, leader of the hounds, sat sleepily in front of his cabin revelling in the warm breeze. Asa stood in his snowy pasture, letting the soft wind blow winter weariness away from his gaunt frame. Danny whistled, and Asa tossed his head up to look around. Danny cast the beam of his light in the direction Asa was looking, and saw Red framed in the black doorway of the mule's shed. Danny whistled again, and the dog ducked into the shed.

Danny plunged through the melting snow to the shed, and entered. Asa's stall, fresh and clean, confronted him. Asa's hay was packed on both sides of the stall, and filled all the rest of the shed. Stretched out, facing the wall and ignoring Danny, Red lay on a forkful of hay that had tumbled from the rack. Danny knelt beside the dog. His fingers tickled Red's ear in that place which the big dog found so difficult to reach with his own hind paw.

"You're actin' like a jug-head," Danny scolded softly. "Come on back to the house, Red."

Red swung his head to look steadily up at Danny, and turned away. Danny flinched. Ross had been right. Red was jealous, fiercely jealous that his beloved master's hands should even stroke another dog, to say nothing of taking her right into the house.

"You're wrong, Red," Danny protested. "I don't like her better'n you. But I got to keep her in the house. She don't know this place like you do, and she don't know yet that she's goin' to belong here. Come on back, Red. You're still king-pin. Come on, Red!"

He ran toward the door, and paused to throw his light back on the hay. Red had stretched full length in it, and did not even raise his head when Danny snapped his fingers and whistled. Danny went worriedly from the shed. Red was deeply insulted, and unless there was some way to atone that insult he would continue to sulk. But—just how might that be done? Danny went back into the cabin to be greeted daintily by Sheilah, who had been lolling against Ross's knees.

"Where is he?" Ross inquired.

"Sleepin' with Asa. He won't come out."

Ross wagged his head. "That dog's a proud 'un. I just dunno what you're goin' to do now."

"He'll come to his senses."

"Yeah?" Ross inquired skeptically. "I'll bet four dollars to an empty shotgun cartridge he never gives in to you."

"But, but he's got to!"

Danny sat down on a chair to stare hard at Sheilah MacGuire. He had wanted a fine dog, a mate for Red, but he had never wanted it to be like this. Red was Red, partridge dog extraordinary and the most satisfactory canine companion that a man could possibly have. If Red was going to stay mad at him why—why he might just as well not have any dog. If he let Sheilah out, and she ran away, she'd probably only go down to Mr. Haggin's. He voiced the thought to Ross.

Ross's mouth tightened sternly, and he shook his

head. "Danny, did you find that dog chasin' 'round in the snow?"

"Why no. But . . ."

"Mr. Haggin ain't goin' to find it thataway, either," Ross pronounced firmly. "Given he'd wanted the dog down to his place, he'd of sent it there. But he sent it to us—to you. If you're not goin' to keep it, you see that he gets it back."

"I was just thinkin'," Danny said miserably. "Maybe we could toll him back with a bait of meat."

"Sure!" Ross scoffed. "You know him better'n that. That Red dog ain't goin' to do nothin' without he wants to."

"I guess you're right," Danny admitted.

Sheilah looked up at Ross, whom she seemed to have adopted as her special mentor, and sighed deeply. She laid her head on Ross's lap, and Ross scratched her ear. Danny sighed unhappily. Sheilah had taken to Ross as Red had taken to him, and now instead of having two dogs he hadn't any. He went to bed, and lay sleepless while the warm zephyrs played outside his window and the long night hours ticked by. A dozen times during the night he reached over the side of his bed for Red, who always slept on a blanket beside him. But the big dog was not there.

The next morning Red emerged from the mule shed and sat in the sun before it. Haggard and worn from lack of sleep, Danny saw him there when he went out to the wood lot for an arm-load of wood, and tried to whistle him into the house. But Red only turned his head toward the sound and looked away again. Danny took his load of wood and his breaking heart back into the house.

"What's he doin' this mornin'?" Ross inquired.

"Settin' by Asa's shed. He won't come to me."

Ross said gently, "Don't let it hit you too hard. I bet he'd like to come back in. But a proud dog's a lot like a proud man."

"If'n he wants to go on bein' a fool he can just be one. I don't care," Danny lied.

"That's the way to take it."

Danny cooked breakfast, and Sheilah went over to sit beside Ross with one paw on his knee as she received tidbits from his plate. Ross finished and pushed his plate back, and a little smile played around his lips as he looked fondly down at the dog. Danny watched, and even in the depths of his own misery found room for surprise. Ross was a man who had always hunted varmints, and preferred varmint hunting dogs. Obviously the delicate Sheilah would never hunt varmints, and maybe not anything, but just the same Ross was engrossed in her.

"Sure is a lot of dog under them red setters' hides," he observed. "We got to let her out to run a bit, Danny."

"Do you think she'll stay here?"

"Sure," Ross said confidently. "I think I can handle this dog. You had the right angle on 'em, Danny. You can't lick such dogs. But they'll do anything for you given they once want to."

He pushed his chair back and opened the door. The

sun had climbed brightly over Stoney Lonesome, and great wet spots appeared on top of the snow. The depressions in the pasture were puddles, and the trunks of the trees gleamed wetly. Sheilah stood for a moment on the porch, and the hounds came out of their kennels to bay at her. She glanced up at Ross, and gave the hounds a wide berth as she padded down the steps. Plainly she lacked Red's bravado—in the first five minutes of his stay at the Pickett household he had shown Mike who was going to be boss of all the dogs there. Ross, a slight smile still on his lips, climbed down the steps with her and followed her about as she cast back and forth in front of the cabin. They started toward the beech woods, and Danny glanced at Red.

He was still sitting by the door of the mule shed, staring indifferently at Sheilah and Ross. Danny let his gaze return to them, and saw Sheilah race toward a clump of brush. Half a dozen partridges burst out of it. Two lit in a hemlock, and the other four scattered in the beech woods. Sheilah raced wildly about, dashing to and fro as she sought to pin down exactly this new and entrancing scent.

"Here, Sheilah," said Ross gently. "Come here, gal."

Sheilah went over and rubbed against Ross's legs. Red left his seat by the mule shed, and at top speed raced across the slush-filled pasture. Danny gasped, and rose to shout. Red had gone mad; he was going to kill this unwelcome trespasser. But he stifled the shout in his throat as Red snapped to a perfect point in front of the hemlocks. He held his point, tail stiff and foreleg curved. Danny dashed in to get his shotgun, and ran across the field.

He heard his father call to him, but paid no attention to it. A hundred feet from Red he stopped running and edged up behind him.

"Get 'em out, Red," he said softly.

Red lunged forward and the two partridges thundered up. Danny raised his gun, deliberately undershot the out-of-season birds, and lowered his shotgun.

"Missed!" he said dejectedly.

Red looked around, his eyes friendly once more and his tail wagging. He looked disdainfully toward the shrinking Sheilah. Red, prince of partridge dogs, had proven himself definitely superior to this puny female, and Danny had witnessed the entire performance. There could not now be the slightest doubt as to which dog was best. He shoved his muzzle deep into Danny's cupped hand and sniffed loudly. Then he went forward to meet Sheilah.

She advanced, uncertain but friendly, and they sniffed noses. Then together they set off toward the house.

CHAPTER 11

OLD MAJESTY

THE SPRING ADVANCED. MELTED SNOW FILLED EVERY little ditch and depression, and the swollen creeks surged over their banks into the meadows and forests around them. Then green grass showed, flowers bloomed, trees were bud-laden, and one day a belated flock of north-bound geese squawked over Stoney Lonesome on their strong-winged passage north. In the shallow little gulley where he had been tearing a log apart to get the white grubs that had burrowed into it, the huge bear raised his long head to watch them go. He licked another white grub from its damp bed, and climbed ponderously out of the gulley.

A quiver, starting at the tip of his almost tailless rear, rolled to the tip of his black snout. A curious light gleamed in his red, pig's eyes, and he ran a pink tongue from the side of his mouth. Suddenly the bear's six hundred and fifty pound body whirled about. He stared back down into the gulley, as though expecting something that should not be, his mad eyes the reflection of his mad brain.

Old Majesty, the huge, the relentless, the savage and unforgiving enemy of every human being in the Wintapi, had come out of hibernation with the first breath of spring, to pad his lean sides with whatever food he could find. But not for him to be contented with spare pickings, or to relinquish the things his shrunken belly craved. Man had not come to him for nearly a year. But he was not afraid to go to man.

He stood up, his shaggy head swung low and his club-like feet braced. He took a few steps forward, and the laurel stalks in front of him crumpled as though their fibrous, tough stems were brittle sticks. The bear kept going, smashing the laurel as he walked straight to the rim of the big plateau. For ten minutes he stood there, swinging his head, gazing into the valley, and smelling the breezes that blew out of it. He quartered down the slope into the gray-trunked beeches that struggled up the hill. Once among them he stopped again.

There was no hurry. The sun was only three-quarters across its westward sky-journey, and there were still hours of daylight. Daylight was not Old Majesty's time when he went among men. Much as he might scorn them, he had a vast respect for their weapons. But when the friendly night clothed the wilderness and made invisible the creatures whose abode it was, man's weapons became almost impotent. Long ago the colossal black bear had learned that man was an ineffective and puny thing at night.

When twilight folded its gray wings over the beech woods he went on, perfectly straight, turning aside for nothing. He knew exactly where he was going because he had been there before, many times, and he would go again whenever the impulse moved him. Old Majesty, unbeaten king of the Wintapi, went where he willed.

He came to the great meadow that enfolded the big Wintapi estate of Mr. Haggin, and stopped just within the protecting forest to examine it. Light gleamed in the houses. The smell of wood smoke tickled his nostrils. With it came the mingled odors of the cattle, sheep, and horses with which Mr. Haggin had stocked his rolling acres. The waiting bear licked his chops. His front feet did a nervous little dance on the ground before him, and an eager whine broke from his half-open mouth. He was king, and the promise of kingly repast was carried to his quivering nostrils on the brisk little wind that blew from the barn to him.

Not until shortly before midnight, when the last light in the last house winked out, did he start across the meadow. He went slowly, cautiously, lifting his huge paws in the short spring grass and putting them carefully back down on the earth. A dog barked, and the huge bear paused to listen intently to it. He advanced again, still not afraid and ready to meet any foe that might come forth to challenge him. But nothing moved. Knowing only the ways of the farm, caring nothing for the forest, the sleeping caretaker whose dog had scented approaching peril awoke to speak angrily. The dog lay down, nervous but afraid to bark again.

Old Majesty padded soft footedly to a corral, and pressed his head against it to peer between the rails. There had been sheep in it that day; their oily scent came heavily to his nostrils and he drooled on the grass. But the sheep had been removed to the security of a barn. Robert Fraley, Mr. Haggin's overseer, had learned his lesson well. Old Majesty had come raiding before, might at any time come again, and nothing must be left outside at night.

The big bear swerved to one of the strong gray barns, and pushed his head against the door. Within he heard cattle stamping nervously, and the threatening rumble of a chained bull that scented danger to the herd. The big bear inserted a front claw in the crevice where the two barn doors rolled shut, and with all his tremendous strength tried to pry them open. But they were stoutly built, and the most he could do was force them an inch apart. Then the oaken doors sprang right back together again. The bear champed his jaws angrily, and slapped the earth in senseless fury. A shower of pebbles leaped up to strike him in the face. His jowl curled in a snarl.

He walked to the sheep fold, and when he could not enter that reared to smash a window with his front paw. Glass tinkled, and the frightened sheep within plunged and milled as they raced to the other end of the fold. Old Majesty settled back to the ground, staring at the houses from which men would come if they came. But still there was no sound. Nothing moved. He reared to thrust his mighty head and shoulders through the broken window, but drew warily back. He could get in. But the barn was a trap. If he was caught within it there was no way out except through the hard-to-enter window. He walked to the horse barn, and the shrill scream of an aroused stallion sliced through the night. Again the stallion screamed.

The big bear swung about, and sat on his haunches facing a house where man had at last awakened. A door creaked open. A lantern gleamed, and came bobbing toward the barn. Old Majesty took a tentative step toward the man, then retreated slowly into the night. Two hundred feet out in the meadow he stopped to watch while the man with the lantern went slowly from one barn to the other. He exclaimed over the broken window, and unlocked the door of the horse barn to go in and quiet the raging stallion. Then, loud and startling in the night, a bell rang. Lights winked on in all the houses, and more lanterns bobbed in the hands of the running men who carried them.

Old Majesty turned and ran back into the beeches. He was still unafraid, still contemptuous of the men, and willing to fight them. But there was no reason for fighting since there was nothing in the big gray barns that he could get. Then, because there had not been, a great rage flooded him. He ran straight up the valley, threading his way among the ponderous beeches, and stopped only when he came to the border of another and smaller clearing.

There was a part-log, part-board cabin nestled in the shadow of some of the huge beech trees. Beside it were four dog kennels, one of them empty, a shed, and a barn. The wind was blowing strongly from the cabin to him, and Old Majesty's lip curled as he read and interpreted the scents it carried. He knew the three hounds within the kennels. They had been on his trail more than once, and he had nothing but scorn for all of them. But as his brain received and placed in their correct categories the scents of the two men and the two dogs in the cabin, his curled lip emitted an ugly snarl.

The only living thing he feared, or respected, was one of the two dogs in the cabin. It was Red, the one dog ever on his trail that he had not been able to outwit or kill. Red had followed him a long way, foiling him at every turn, and after a long chase had bayed him on a rock. One of the men in the cabin had come with a gun. But Old Majesty had escaped. His head drooped so low that his black snout almost touched the ground.

A gaunt mule rested in the pasture that surrounded the shed. Old Majesty's head swung further around, and his beady little eyes fastened on the mule. His hunt had been frustrated, but here was prey surrounded by no oaken barn. The big bear threw caution away and began to run.

Instantly everything about the cabin came awake. As one the three chained hounds emerged from their kennels and cast themselves again and again to the ends of their chains, falling down and getting up to leap again. The two dogs in the cabin added their barking to the din, and a light glowed. There were no stolid farmers in this cabin, but woodsmen who knew the ways of the woods.

Old Majesty plunged on, and now that he had started nothing would turn him aside. He crashed through the wire fence as though it were paper. The terrified mule swung to gallop away. But the black shadow that raced through the night was beside it, and reared to strike its thin neck with a sledge-hammer paw. For one brief second, with jaws stretched wide, the mule tried to fight back. The bear struck again, and the mule went to its knees. It rolled over on its back with all four legs moving feebly.

The beam of a flash-light stabbed the darkness, and from the porch of the cabin red streaks flashed as two rifles spat their leaden messengers into the night. Old Majesty's hind paw whipped up to strike at his right ear, through which a bullet had passed. He ran around the mule shed, putting it between himself and the riflemen, and went into the beech woods. For a moment he stopped, sitting on his haunches and facing the cabin as though half-minded to go back and renew the fight. But, cutting through the bedlam created by the baying hounds and the hysterically screeching Sheilah, Red's battle challenge came steadily. With feet shuffling and head swinging Old Majesty climbed through the beech woods back up Stoney Lonesome's slope.

Daylight found him far back in the wilderness. He had stopped to dig a woodchuck from its hole, and had eaten it. Also, he had torn apart more logs and filled his belly with grubs. Having eaten, he sought a hemlock thicket and curled up to sleep. But he awoke in the soft gray of early morning and sat up on his haunches, straining his ears to catch again the sound he thought he had heard. It came, the silvery, far-off baying of hounds. Five minutes later the big bear knew that they were on his trail. He snapped his jaws, angry because they were, and walked out of the thicket into the wild forest beyond. When the yelling hounds were heard more clearly, and had closed the distance between them, he ran.

All day, alternately running and walking, he travelled across the top of Stoney Lonesome and into the unnamed wilderness beyond it. And all day he heard the baying hounds. The bear's jaws gaped wide, his tongue lolled from the side of his mouth. Long, greasy strings of slaver swung from his jaws. And, as his weariness increased, so did his anger.

Night came, and the yelling dogs ceased their noise. From the summit of a high and brush-covered peak, Old Majesty turned to survey the wilderness through which he had run. Far below, in a valley, something shone brightly yellow. It was the campfire of the man who had come with the dogs. Ross Pickett was taking no chances on his hounds meeting Old Majesty in the dark. But they would meet him, and he would meet him. Asa had been killed. And, though only another four-footed one, Asa had been Ross Pickett's friend.

Again, with the first faint streak of dawn, Old Majesty heard the dogs yelling on his trail. He left the thicket where he had bedded, ran up and over the mountain and down the other side. The country was wild here, a desolate, lost place whose solitude was rarely broken by the advent of man or the sound of his guns. Forest fire had swept it years ago, and the trunks of the big hardwoods that had clothed it lay supine on the ground or stretched withered skeletons toward the sky. A lush growth of small pines had replaced the hardwoods. Huge boulders lay tumbled all about. All morning Old Majesty ran through them. The sun was directly overhead when, at last, he decided that he would run no more.

He stopped in front of a boulder as big as a house, and backed against it. Rising on his hind legs, he swung his front ones right, left, and forward, as though to assure himself that he would have plenty of room in which to fight when fighting became necessary. He listened, his head bent forward. Then a cunning gleam flicked across his red eyes and he dropped to all fours.

He swung into the pines, at a right angle to the trail he had made coming in, and after walking seventy feet swung to parallel it. Moving slowly, careful to rustle no twig and break no branch whose sound might betray him, he stalked through the pines back to the trail and lay beside it. He heard the hounds yelling nearer, then saw them come in sight. Old Majesty lay very still, and when the three hounds were right in front of him he sprang.

His huge body overwhelmed Old Mike, bore him down and into the earth. The grizzled old hound, veteran of a hundred hunts, wriggled and tried to bring his jaws into play. But Old Majesty moved very carefully, feeling beneath his breast with his mighty front paw. His claws encountered and sank into Old Mike's neck, and he dragged the fighting hound into the open. He slapped with his free paw, and Old Mike's back sagged. The old hound dragged himself forward with his front feet. His open jaws closed on Old Majesty's flank. The big bear slapped again, and Mike died as it had from the first been inevitable that he would die. But his jaws were clamped shut, and in them was a long strip of Old Majesty's skin.

Then the bear swung to deal with the hysterically yelling pups. They separated, one going to the side while the other feinted from the front. Old Majesty moved slowly, slapping at the dog in front of him and watching it keep just out of range. Suddenly and unexpectedly he whirled, and his slashing paw pounded the neck of the pup that was boring in from the side. The hound flew ten feet through the air and collided soddenly with a boulder. Old Majesty leaped ahead, trapping the other pup between his front paws and pounding it into a bloody pulp. For ten minutes, in delirious, unreasoning rage, he hammered the three dogs. From far off he heard the man shout.

"Halloo-ooo!"

Old Majesty rose to listen, his little eyes very bright and his ears alert. The lust of battle still gripped him, and victory was his. He backed into the brush and stood very quietly waiting. The breeze brought Ross Pickett's scent to him before he saw anything. Carrying his rifle in his right hand, Ross came running toward that place where he had last heard the dogs. Old Majesty lunged and struck, once.

But fighting a man was very different from fighting a dog, and the big bear knew it. Despite his anger he was nervous, and he did not time his charge with the same split-second precision that had taken the hounds to their deaths. His front paw struck Ross Pickett's left arm, glanced off his chest, and sent him spinning into the pines. But Ross kept hold of his rifle, and dropped to a sitting position with it in his right hand. He cocked it with his thumb, and raised it with his right arm.

About to follow up his charge, Old Majesty paused. He had lived to be old because he knew many things, and among them was the certainty that a man with a gun, in broad daylight, was more than a match for himself. After split-second indecision he turned and ran back into the pines, while Ross's bullet whistled over him.

Down at the cabin in the beech woods, Danny Pickett sat in the warm sunshine. Red was beside him, and Sheilah lay outstretched on the soft grass. Danny glanced fondly at her. Sheilah was with pups, due to litter in a very few days, and now could take no violent exercise and must be very careful. Somebody had to stay at the house and watch her while Ross and his hounds were up in the mountains on Old Majesty's trail.

Danny looked at the heap of brown earth that covered Asa, and lifted his eyes to the mountains. An anxious frown creased his brow, and uneasiness gnawed within him. But nothing could have stopped Ross's going on this hunt, and nothing could have persuaded him to take anyone with him. Old Majesty had killed Asa, and Ross must conduct a deadly, personal feud with any varmint that harmed anything about the Pickett household. Probably the hounds would not bay Old Majesty—no hounds ever had. But they were certainly giving him a run. Ross had been gone for three days now.

Danny's gaze strayed back to Sheilah, and something deep within him stirred. The indistinct vision that he had tried to see clearly ever since the dog show sought to assume shape and form. But somehow it would not, although it seemed to concern Sheilah directly. Danny knew only that in the back of his mind there lived a fine dog, a magnificent dog, a dog to put all others to shame. But weren't Red and Sheilah all that? He walked down the steps and knelt to tickle Sheilah's ear.

"How you feelin'?" he crooned. "You're goin' to have

a big litter, then you and me and the pups and Red, we're all goin' to do great things."

Red sat suddenly up, head erect and ears alert. A short, challenging bark rumbled from him, and Danny raised his head to follow the dog's gaze. He gasped. Ross came out of the beech woods into the clearing. He was walking very slowly, his eyes on the ground and his left arm limp at his side. Danny raced across the pasture to meet him, passed an arm about his father's shoulders.

"Pappy!"

"I met the bear," Ross Pickett said wearily. "He got the dogs, all three of 'em."

"Don't talk now, Pappy."

Danny guided his father into the cabin, took off his clothes and put him to bed. He held a glass of water to his father's lips, laid a cool towel across his hot forehead. Then, with Red racing beside him, he ran down the Smokey Creek trail to Mr. Haggin's. Curley Jordan, one of the caretakers, met him.

"Call Doc Smedley!" Danny snapped. "Get him here quick! Pappy's been hurt by a bear!"

He ran back up the trail, and into the cabin. Ross lay quietly on the bed. But there was misery and heartbreak in his eyes, and he was staring blankly at the ceiling. Danny glanced at his blood-stained shirt, and stared back at Ross. Curley Jordan ran in, and an hour later Dr. Smedley followed. He bent over Ross, while Danny hovered solicitously in the background and watched him work. Dr. Smedley straightened.

"Is he . . . Is he bad hurt?" Danny gulped.

"Three broken ribs and a broken arm," Dr. Smedley said. "That's quite a smash. But he'll be all right."

Dr. Smedley filled a hypodermic, and made ready to inject it into Ross's shoulder.

"What's that for?" Danny asked.

"To put him to sleep. He won't feel it when we set the broken bones, and he needs a rest."

Danny stepped to the bed, and looked down on Ross's pain-distorted face.

"Pappy, where'd you leave that big bear's track?"

"In all them little pines what grew up where the fire went," Ross whispered. "You can't miss it, Danny. Cross three cricks off to the west of Stoney Lonesome, and climb that big mountain where we got the fisher out of the cave two years gone. It's on a straight line between a dead chestnut on the east side of that mountain, and a big pine on the west side of the next. It's the only big pine there. Hit right between 'em and you can't miss. He got all the dogs, Danny. All of 'em. Be careful."

"I will, Pappy. Don't fret."

He stepped back and watched Dr. Smedley inject the anesthetic into Ross's arm. Ross dropped into an easy slumber, and Danny turned to Curley Jordan.

"Will you stay here with Sheilah and Pappy, until I come back?"

"Gosh yes, Danny. I'll be glad to, and Mr. Haggin would want me to. What are you going to do?"

"There ain't but one dog ever bayed Old Majesty," Danny Pickett said grimly. "And that dog can do it again. I'll be seein' you when Red and I get him!"

CHAPTER 12

TROPHY FOR RED

DANNY DIDN'T LOOK AGAIN AT ANY OF THE MEN IN THE cabin. He took a canvas packsack from its hanger, packed into it a box of matches, a slab of bacon, a small package of coffee, five pounds of flour, two loaves of bread, and a first-aid kit. He hung a sheathed knife at his belt, put a box of cartridges in his pocket, took his gun from its rack, loaded it, and was ready for the Wintapi wilderness. Red trotted soberly over to sit beside him, and followed closely when Danny went out on the porch.

He stood there, feeling the warm spring breezes blow about his face and neck and ruffle his shirt. And it seemed to him that never before in his entire life had he been so calm, or known so exactly just what he was going to do.

Old Majesty must die, he was very sure of that. Not alone because he had killed Asa and hurt Ross, and probably would hurt or kill other men, but for an added reason. The Wintapi was wild and hard—ever ready with its threats and dangers. Only those who could meet and parry its blows were entitled to live there, or could live there. Now Old Majesty had asserted his own supremacy over all of it, in attacking Ross had proclaimed that nothing could walk in the Wintapi unless he willed it. And Danny knew that he must meet the big bear's challenge, must go into the mountains and fight Old Majesty on his own grounds. This was not something that a man could forget or run from.

At the same time, he was fully aware of the risks he ran and the chances he took. First there was Red, the dog that, next to Ross, he loved better than anything else. In hunting Old Majesty Red might be killed. Or, if he was not killed or even hurt, the fact that Danny must urge him to hunt a bear, a varmint, could easily make meaningless all the long hours that Danny had taken to teach him to hunt partridges alone. Lastly, Danny considered the fact that he himself might be hurt.

But he still knew that he had to go, that Ross expected him to go. Ross saw the Wintapi as Danny did, and knew that he who quailed at any challenge it hurled was forever lost. Danny bit his lip. He was young, but old enough to know that life was seldom easy. And it seemed to him that in the future there would be a great many other bears to meet. How he met them depended in great measure on what he did now with Old Majesty. It had become his fight. Regardless of loss or sacrifice he must give everything to winning it.

He walked down the porch steps, averted his eyes from the dog kennels, and walked across the pasture into the beech woods. The sun sprayed its golden rays through their budding twigs, painted the forest floor beneath them. Red crowded close to his side, seeming in some mysterious way to know that this was no ordinary trip. Even when he reached the crest of Stoney Lonesome Danny did not turn his eyes back for one last look at the cabin.

Danny walked around the rim of the big plateau, keeping out of the laurel that grew upon it in the scrub. There was no special hurry. Ross had left the scene of the battle yesterday afternoon, and since had been making his pain-racked journey home. Certainly he would no longer find a fresh trail away from that place where Old Majesty had killed the hounds, and he might be in the mountains many days before he had the final reckoning with the big bear. But he had to stay, and would stay, until the final hour of that reckoning.

Twilight fell, and Danny stopped beside a brawling little stream that tumbled down a wild mountain valley. He took a line and fishhook from the pack, turned over a rock and picked up the worms that crawled in the damp earth beneath it, and caught eight of the shining little brook trout that swarmed in the stream and nibbled eagerly at his proffered bait. He broiled them on a stick, shared them with Red, and moved his fire to face a huge boulder. Sitting with his back to the boulder, he stared into the flames and caressed Red. And there in the still night it was as though some mysterious vessel poured into him a renewal of an old faith. First it was faith in himself, and then that in Red. His first judgment of the big setter had been that here was a dog with heart, courage and brain, as well as beauty and near perfection. Somehow he knew now that that judgment had been the correct one.

He was awake with the first streaks of dawn, had caught and cooked more trout and started up the valley. Danny climbed the lost ridge at its head, and struck into the big pines that lined the ridge. The small pines wherein Ross and his hounds had had their tragic meeting with Old Majesty were scarcely two hours away. A warm wind eddied down the ridge to blow against his face, and Danny strode briskly. A pulsing eagerness crept through him, and he gripped the rifle more firmly. Red ranged out to hunt through a copse of brush at one side, and came running back.

Danny climbed the mountain where he and Ross had taken a snarling, spitting fisher from a cave two years before, and walked to its east slope to stand directly under what had been a fine chestnut tree. Now its branches were leafless and gray, its twigs broken and shapeless. He looked directly across the valley that yawned beneath him at a huge pine growing on the slope of the opposite mountain. The wind, playing up the valley, rippled the tops of the smaller pines down there and coaxed a soft song from them. Danny's roving eye laid out a straight line between the chestnut stub and the big pine, and in the valley below him he saw a cruising crow plane out of the air into the little pines. From the end of the valley another crow cawed raucously, and presently came winging down to alight where the first had descended. That was where the hounds lay.

Danny's eyes marked the spot from which he would have to start. Some day he would return, give what was left of Old Mike and the two pups a suitable burial, and mark something on their grave about the battle they had had. But that must wait. They had to be avenged first.

Danny sat beneath the chestnut stub, an arm about Red's neck and the rifle resting where he could instantly reach and bring it into play. His brow wrinkled in deep thought. He could go down into the valley, and work out Old Majesty's trail from the place where he had fought. But that might take hours or even days of painstaking effort.

"Where would he go, Red?" Danny asked softly. "Where would that old hellion of gone from here?"

Red whined, and turned his head to lick Danny's ear. Danny stared hard at the ground, saw a worm inching along it, and snapped his head erect. Insect eggs were hatching in the dead, damp logs, and they'd be full of grubs. Having failed in his bold attempt to raid the farms, Old Majesty had to take his living from the wilderness. And, at this season of the year, grubs were the most plentiful and easiest-to-get food in it.

Danny bent his head forward and closed his eyes, trying in his mind to reconstruct a picture of the country as he knew it. Certainly Old Majesty, bold enough to ambush the three hounds and Ross, had not fled in blind panic when he left the scene of the battle. Probably he had even waited around to see if he was going to be followed any more. But he had had a long run, and would want to rest and eat after it. Two mountains away there were a great many fallen trees whose trunks were moss-encrusted and whose pulp was dozey. Danny flipped a penny, and when it fell heads-up rose to quarter down the mountain. Before trying to work out a stale track he would cross those two mountains and see if he could not find a fresh one.

Red padded behind him as he toiled up one mountain, down its other side, and up the mountain beyond. He paused on the summit to stare down the slope. Red edged around him, pricked up his ears, and raised his hackles. He growled, looked up and wagged his tail.

Danny squatted down, and clamped his hand over the big dog's muzzle as he strove to see past the trees in front of him. Wind shook a copse of brush, and Danny brought his rifle up with one hand on the breech, ready to cock it and shoot. He rose and walked slowly down the slope, passing the yellow, ripped stumps that marched in endless lines along it and threading his way among the prostrate tree trunks. Some had been shredded by powerful claws; a bear had been at them.

It was where a little spring bubbled out of the mountain side and softened the earth about it that Danny found Old Majesty's track. He knelt to examine it, a huge thing longer than his own foot and wider than his spread hand. His guess then, had been the correct one; Old Majesty had come here to feast on grubs. The track by the spring was scarcely two hours old. Danny grasped Red by the scruff of the neck, and shoved his nose down in the track.

"That's him," he said. "That's the varmint we got to find."

Red sniffed long and deeply at the track, and raised his head to look at Danny. He sat down, tail flat on the ground behind him, staring down the slope. Danny watched. Red never had been a trailing dog, and would not now become one. But if he could catch the body scent of Old Majesty, and was urged to the attack, he would chase the big bear and finally bring it to bay. Danny climbed back to the summit of the mountain and sat down. The wind was almost straight out of the west, blowing gently but steadily. Clouds scudded across the sky, and the feathered tips of the pine trees bent. For a long while Danny stared steadily into the valley, and looked from it to Red.

Old Majesty was not there now or Red would smell him and indicate his presence. But there was no sign that he had been alarmed and knew that another pursuer was on his trail. Danny looked back down to the spring where he had found the track. He could follow the trail if he wanted to, and eventually work it out, but he must wage a battle of wits as well as one of scientific woodcraft. Fresh as it was, it would still take a long while to puzzle out that trail on the hard, rocky ground. Danny looked again down the slope, at the vast number of decaying logs that lay undisturbed. All of them were full of grubs, and if Old Majesty wanted to rest a few days he would not stray far from this place. Probably he was resting now, and not far away. But exactly where was he and what was the best way to go about finding him?

Danny rose, and with Red padding beside him travelled straight up the top of the mountain. He crossed the valley at its head, crossed the next mountain to the one beyond, and swung down it. He came off its sloping nose into a forested valley, and struck due east. But all the while he had been both studying the ground beneath him and watching Red. The big setter had stalked away three or four times to hunt partridges that he had scented in the thickets. But not once had his nose gone to the ground, and Danny had seen no bear track leading away. Old Majesty, then, was somewhere within the circle he had made.

Danny walked due east, crossing the noses of the mountains whose heads he had walked around and returned to the foot of the slope where the grub-ridden logs lay. He walked around it, up the valley that separated it from the next hill, and again sat down to ponder. He ate bread smeared with bacon grease, gave Red some, and sat down with his back against a boulder. Twilight came, and erratic bats swooped up and down the little stream before him. But pitch darkness had descended on the wilderness before Danny started up the mountain again.

He left his pack beside the stream, carrying only a three-cell flash-light and his rifle as he climbed. The wind still blew steadily from the west. A whip-poor-will shrieked, and Red halted to peer toward the sound. Danny waited for the big dog to catch up with him. He was still a hundred feet below the mountain's crest when he stooped to crawl.

The back of his neck tingled, and little shivers ran up and down his spine. Old Majesty, just twice in his whole terrible career, had been seen in daylight by men who carried rifles. Ross had missed his shot, and Danny had dared not shoot for fear that a wounded bear might injure Red. But, though the big bear had been hunted many times by day, as far as Danny knew this was the first time anyone had ever thought of stalking him by night. He reached the summit of the mountain, and felt in the darkness for Red. His fingers found and clenched the big dog's fur.

Almost imperceptibly he felt Red stiffen, and Danny laid the rifle across his knees while his other hand stole forth to clamp about the big setter's muzzle. He thrilled

with pride. Again his guess had been the right one. Old
Majesty had not wandered away, but after eating his
fill of grubs had merely gone to sleep in some secluded
thicket. Now he was back. From down the slope came
the ripping sound of another log being torn apart. Then
an eerie silence.

It was broken by the buzz of an insect in a nearby
tree, and Danny snapped his head erect. A light wind
blew out of the valley. Red maintained his tense stance.
The wind eddied around, blowing from all directions,
and Red shrank close to the earth. A clammy hand
brushed Danny's spine. He let go of the dog's muzzle to
pick up his rifle. He clutched it very tightly, wrapping
his fingers about the breech with one hand on the trigger. Something was happening out there in the darkness,
something that only Red could interpret, and in that
moment Danny knew that he was afraid.

Red turned his head, and held it poised while he remained rooted in his tracks. Slowly he swung his body
about, facing up the ridge now instead of into the valley.
Inch by inch he continued to turn, facing down the other
side of the razor-backed ridge, and swinging until he
had made a complete circle and was staring into the valley again. Then, Danny understood. He bit his lip so
hard that he felt the taste of blood in his mouth, and let
go of Red's ruff to reach into his pocket for the flash-
light.

They were hunting Old Majesty, but there in the black
night the great bear was also hunting them. He had
come back to feed on the grubs in the dead logs, scented

Danny and Red, and rather than run again had elected to try conclusions in the darkness, the time that he favored most and that was most favorable to him. Danny swallowed hard as the complete realization of that was driven home to him, but he grasped it perfectly. Old Majesty was no ordinary bear, but bigger, wiser, fiercer, and more intelligent than any other bear that Danny had ever known. Beyond a doubt he remembered Red, and that Red had once brought him to bay. Even though he might now fear the dog, he still knew that he would have to fight it out sooner or later, and was selecting that fight to his own advantage.

In the darkness he had walked clear around them, nerving himself to the attack and trying to choose the best method for it. Now he was just a little way down the hill, looking them over, reading them with his nose and listening for their next move. Danny drew back the hammer of his rifle, and in the night its metallic little click was startlingly loud. He held it in his right hand, clutching the flash-light with his left, and spoke softly,

"Stay here, Red. Stay with me."

Down the slope pebbles rattled, and there was the scraping of a claw on a rock. Danny thought hard, trying in his mind to reconstruct an exact picture of the mountain side as he had seen it earlier that morning. The nearest big rock, he thought, was about sixty yards from where they stood now and Old Majesty must have walked on it. Half-tempted to flash the light and shoot, he hesitated. The bear might come nearer, present a fairer shot. If he did not, if instead of attacking he chose

to run, Danny could always urge Red forward to follow him. Somewhere in the lost wilderness Red would once again bring Old Majesty to bay.

Red was once more facing up the ridge, and had taken two stiff-legged steps forward. Danny poised the flashlight and rifle. Red did not turn his head again, so the bear was standing still. Danny snapped the light on. Its white beam travelled into the night to fall like a silver cage about something huge and black, something that stood scarcely twenty yards up the spine of the ridge. The wind blowing out of the valley eddied around it, curled the long hair that hung from its belly.

Danny raised the gun, supported it on the hand in which he gripped the light, and aimed in its uncertain glow. This, he thought, was not real or right. It was something that you did only in a dream, and awoke to find it a blurred memory. But the cold trigger about which his finger curled was real enough, as was the crack of the rifle and the little tongue of red flame that licked into the darkness. He heard the sodden little 'splot' as the bullet struck and buried itself in flesh. Red's battle roar rang through the night, and at almost exactly the same second the big dog and Old Majesty launched themselves at each other.

Danny shot again and again, desperately working the lever of his gun and pumping bullet after bullet into the oncoming black mass. A feeling of hopelessness almost overwhelmed him. The bear kept coming. It was as though Old Majesty was a monstrous thing, an animated mass of something that had no more life than a stone or a rock, and upon which bullets had no effect. Wide-eyed, Danny saw it within thirty, then twenty feet of him, and in that moment he knew that he would have died if it had not been for Red.

The big setter met the charging bear, and closed with him. Old Majesty's paw flashed, raked down the dog's chest, and Red reeled away to roll over and over on the ground. His attention diverted from Danny, Old Majesty lunged after the dog.

Danny shook his head. He seemed still to be in a dream, in the throes of something terrible from which sane awakening only could release him. Feverishly he found himself ripping the box of cartridges apart, pumping more bullets into the rifle's magazine. His legs seemed to belong to someone else as he ran forward through the night, held the muzzle of his gun within two feet of Old Majesty's ear, and pulled the trigger. The big bear jerked convulsively, quivered, and settled down to stretch his great length on the earth.

For a moment Danny stood pale and trembling, the gun dangling by his side and the flash-light painting the unreal scene before him. He saw Red, whose coat was now stained with crimson, rise on three legs and prepare to renew the battle. He lunged at the bear, but stopped and turned toward Danny, his jaws very wide open, panting hard. Danny faltered, the rifle clattered to the ground, and tears rolled unashamed from his eyes. Red was everything Danny had thought him and very much more. Beautiful, courageous, strong—and noble. He would fight to the death if need be, but would not molest or disgrace a fallen enemy. Danny snapped back to reality.

"Red!"

The cry was wrenched from him. He ran forward to kneel beside the wounded dog. His hand strayed to Red's left chest and leg. Blood trickled through his fingers as he felt torn flesh and muscles. Even as he turned the light on, he knew that Red would never win another prize in a dog show. His left front leg was ripped half away. Danny picked the dog up, and carried him down the mountain to where he had left the pack. He knelt beside him, dusted the gaping wounds with sulfa powder, and wrapped a clean white bandage around them. Danny took off his jacket, made of it a soft bed for the big setter, and built a fire.

Morning came slowly. The sun strove to break through the mists that blanketed the valley, and the little stream ran quarrelsomely on. Red lay stiffly on the coat, but raised his head to grin and wagged his tail in the dawn's dim light. Danny unwrapped the blood-soaked bandage and looked at the wound. There was no infection. But it would be a long time before Red was able to travel. Danny rigged his fishline, and caught trout in the little stream. In the middle of the afternoon he climbed back up the mountain, and looked at the still form of Old Majesty. Danny shuddered. Even now, if it was not for that giant, quiet thing, last night would be like a dream. But let the bear lie where it was, let it remain, a fallen king, in the wilderness it had once ruled.

Day followed day as they camped by the little stream.

Red got up from his bed to walk stiffly about, and Danny watched with his heart in his eyes. Red's wounds were healing well, but an ugly scar showed and he would never again have much use of his left front leg. Danny gathered the dog to him, and hugged Red very tightly.

On the eighth day, with Red limping behind him, he started down the valley toward home. They camped that night in another little valley, under the shadow of Stoney Lonesome's laurel thickets. With Red's fine head pillowed on his lap, Danny sat before the leaping little fire he had built and stared into the darkness. Somehow he seemed to have changed. The old Danny Pickett had gone forth on the outlaw bear's trail, but a new one was returning. And the new one was a Danny Pickett able to do what he never could have done before.

Late the next afternoon they broke out of the beech woods into the clearing and saw the shanty. Danny stopped, and his left hand strayed down to rest on the big setter's head. Ross stood on the porch. But that gray-haired, crisp man dressed in sports tweeds who was at the foot of the steps talking with Ross could be none other than Mr. Haggin. Danny shook his head wonderingly. The old Danny Pickett would have been terrified at bringing Mr. Haggin's dog back as he was bringing Red. But the new Danny seemed able to do it, to cope with and meet this problem just as he could cope with others. He walked slowly across the pasture toward the shanty. And for some reason that, too, seemed to have undergone a change. Asa and the four hounds were gone. Ross, Sheilah, Red, and himself, remained. That

fact alone seemed to have brought about the trans-
formation.

Danny's glance paused briefly on the sling in which
his father's left arm rested, then strayed to Ross's face.

"Where is he?" Ross asked.

"Dead," Danny said. "Dead up on a ridge. We met
him in the night. Red and me killed him in the dark."

Ross nodded. "Good thing," he murmured.

Danny swung to face the stern-visaged Mr. Haggin.
Red pressed very closely against his legs, and Danny's
dangling hand rested on the big dog's head.

"I did it," he said. "It's my fault and mine alone. I let
him get at the bear. If I hadn't of taken him along, he
wouldn't of been hurt. But I did take him along and he
is hurt; he'll never go to another show. He's spoiled for
you. But he's never spoiled for me and never will be. If
you'll sell me Red I'll pay you every cent of the seven
thousand dollars he cost you."

He heard and paid no attention to Ross's incredulous
gasp. Something strong seemed to have grown within
him. He was not the Danny Pickett who had been born
and lived in poverty all his life. He had cast off the old
shackles, the confining bonds that said he and Ross had
to struggle along as best they could. If others could do
big things so could he.

"I haven't got seven thousand dollars and you know I
haven't. But I can get it—in time I can get it. And I've
got to have Red; I can't part with him. He's got to be
mine. And I tell you again that I'll give you every cent
you paid for him if only you'll sell him to me!"

Mr. Haggin said suddenly and unexpectedly, "That's a reasonable enough offer and I'll accept it. But in one way you're thinking like a fool."

"Why?"

"Because a man was hurt by that bear. If he hurt one man in time he'd kill another, and no matter how valuable it might be, any man's life is still worth more than any animal's. If you had to have Red to help you hunt that bear down you did right taking him and you know it."

"I thought the same thing."

"Then whatever led you to believe that I'd think otherwise? Furthermore, Danny, it's good business for me to sell you that dog. He's won best of breed, and will never win best of show simply because he isn't quite good enough. Then there are little matters like stud fees. You can put him out at stud for fifty or seventy-five dollars, and any breeder in the country with a good bitch will be glad to pay it. Of course, if you don't want the fee you can usually take your pick of the resulting litter. By the way, now that you have more responsibilities, I'm raising you to a hundred dollars a month. I'll hold back fifty, and apply it on what you owe me for Red. About next year, if everything works out the way I think it will, you can name your own salary. Men really capable of handling a dog aren't easy to find, and even if we can't take Red back we can show Sheilah again this year. I want you to take her into the ring, but maybe we'll let Bob handle the pup if we enter one."

"Pup?" Danny was still dazed.

Mr. Haggin grinned. "How do you like Sheilah, Danny?"

"She's a wonderful dog."

"Your dad thinks so too. He . . ."

"I told him I'd allus been a hound man," Ross admitted a trifle sheepishly. "But that Sheilah, doggone her hide! She's an awful lot of dog. I asked Mr. Haggin if he minded if I sort of worked with you on these setters 'stead of gettin' more hounds. Not that I'm ever goin' to forget Mike and those pups. But these setters . . . I ain't askin' no pay."

Mr. Haggin winked at Danny. "He might even be worth a salary when we get a really big string of setters, eh? Dr. Dan MacGruder went abroad, Danny; took a post in China. He hadn't any good place to leave Sheilah, so he sold her to me dirt cheap. But come on, Danny, we have something to show you." He grinned again. "Just remember that you didn't own Red until a few minutes ago, so we'll sort of have to work together on this. Of course the next time you can have your pick of the litter."

Danny followed Ross and Mr. Haggin around the corner of the shanty, and came upon Sheilah stretched out in the warm sun. She raised a proud head to look at them, and wagged her tail in happy greeting to Red. Danny stared, spellbound.

Five blunt-nosed puppies all snuggled contentedly against their mother's flank. But one, a little bigger and stronger than the rest, raised his head when he heard unaccustomed noise. And, puppy though he was, even now there was about him an invisible but very definite aura of the essence that Danny knew as quality. It was as though the tiny mite of dogdom had inherited all the finest qualities of both his father and mother, and in so doing was just a little finer than either one. Danny smiled, very happily, and in the tiny pup saw the incarnation of all the dreams that had troubled him since he had first begun to appreciate a fine throroughbred dog.

But in the back of his mind still another and even more indistinct vision already seemed to be crowding the first. The tiny pup was only one step forward, and there would be many, many more.

Red walked stiffly up. His tail wagged as he sniffed noses with Sheilah, and looked carefully at his two sons and three daughters.

THE AUTHOR

Although Jim Kjelgaard likes to have his name pronounced in the Danish way, Kyell' guard, his boyhood was as American as Tom Sawyer's. A great grandson of the man who brought the family name from Denmark, he was born in New York City in 1910, but grew up on a mountain farm in the famous Black Forest region of north-central Pennsylvania. Here, surrounded by forest-covered mountains cut by game trails and trout streams, he and his four brothers lived a rugged, outdoor life, and grew up wise in the ways of the woods. The year he graduated from high school, Jim and another boy spent a season on their own in the wilderness, hunting and trapping. After that, the world of business held little attraction.

Jim had been writing since the age of ten. When he finally sold a story for five hundred dollars, he determined to become a free-lance writer. His interests had always been the out-of-doors and American history. So it was natural that his first book, Forest Patrol, should be a story centered on the adventures of a young forest ranger, which the author had known at first hand. His second book, Rebel Siege, is an historical tale of frontier life during the Revolution. Big Red is his third book.

Jim Kjelgaard now makes his home in Milwaukee, from which he and his equally outdoor wife make as many expeditions to the wilds as possible. Small daughter Karen can't quite keep up with her parents yet, but she's learning fast.